STEPHEN CRANE'S

THE RED BADGE OF COURAGE

THE GRAPHIC NOVEL

adapted by Wayne Vansant

PUFFIN BOOKS

PUFFIN BOOKS

Published by the Penguin Group

Penguin Young Readers Group,

345 Hudson Street, New York, NY 10014 U.S.A.

Penguin Group (Canada). 10 Alcorn Avenue, Toronto, Ontario, Canada M4V 3B2
(a division of Pearson Penguin Canada Inc.)

Penguin Books Ltd, 80 Strand, London WC2R 0RL, England

Penguin Ireland, 25 St. Stephen's Green, Dublin 2, Ireland
(a division of Penguin Books Ltd)

Penguin Group (Australia), 250 Camberwell Road, Camberwell, Victoria 3124,
Australia (a division of Pearson Australia Group Pty Ltd)

Penguin Books India Pvt Ltd, 11 Community Centre, Panchsheel Park,
New Delhi – 110 017, India

Penguin Group (NZ), Cnr Airborne and Rosedale Roads, Albany, Auckland 1310,
New Zealand (a division of Pearson New Zealand Ltd)

Penguin Books (South Africa) (Pty) Ltd, 24 Sturdee Avenue, Rosebank,
Johannesburg 2196, South Africa

Registered Offices: Penguin Books Ltd, 80 Strand, London WC2R 0RL, England

First published by Puffin Books, a division of Penguin Young Readers Group, 2005

10 9 8 7 6 5 4 3 2 1

A Byron Preiss Book
Byron Preiss Visual Publications
24 West 25th Street, New York, NY 10010

Adapted by Wayne Vansant
Cover art by Don Troiani
Series Editor: Dwight Jon Zimmerman
Series Assistant Editor: April Isaacs
Interior Design by M. Postawa & Gilda Hannah
Cover Design by M. Postawa

Puffin Books ISBN 0-14-240410-1

Printed in the United States of America

STEPHEN CRANE'S

THE RED BADGE
OF COURAGE

THE COLD PASSED RELUCTANTLY FROM THE EARTH, AND THE RETIRING FOG REVEALED AN ARMY STRETCHED OUT ON THE HILLS, RESTING.

AS THE LANDSCAPE CHANGED FROM BROWN TO GREEN, THE ARMY AWAKENED, AND BEGAN TO TREMBLE WITH EAGERNESS AT THE NOISE OF RUMORS.

WE'RE GOIN' T' MOVE T'MORRAH SURE...

WE'RE GOIN' WAY UP RIVER, CUT ACROSS, AN' COME AROUND BEHINT 'EM.

5

TO HIS ATTENTIVE AUDIENCE THE TALL SOLDIER DREW A LOUD AND ELABORATE PLAN OF A VERY BRILLIANT CAMPAIGN. WHEN HE FINISHED, THE BLUE-COATED MEN SCATTERED INTO SMALL ARGUING GROUPS BETWEEN THE ROWS OF SQUAT BROWN HUTS AND TENTS.

A LOUD PRIVATE TOOK THE MATTER AS AN AFFRONT.

IT'S A LIE, THAT'S ALL IT IS A THUNDERIN' LIE. I DON'T BELIEVE THE DERNED OLD ARMY'S EVER GOING TO MOVE.

WE'RE SET. I'VE GOT READY TO MOVE EIGHT TIMES IN THE LAST TWO WEEKS, AND WE AIN'T MOVED YET.

THE TALL SOLDIER FELT CALLED UPON TO DEFEND THE TRUTH OF A RUMOR HE HIMSELF HAD INTRODUCED. HE AND THE LOUD ONE CAME NEAR TO FIGHTING OVER IT.

MANY OF THE MEN ENGAGED IN A SPIRITED DEBATE. ONE OUTLINED IN A PECULIARLY LUCID MANNER ALL THE PLANS OF THE COMMANDING GENERAL.

HE WAS OPPOSED BY MEN WHO ADVOCATED THAT THERE WERE OTHER PLANS OF. CAMPAIGN.

THEY CLAMORED AT EACH OTHER, NUMBERS MAKING FUTILE BIDS FOR THE POPULAR ATTENTION.

THERE WAS A YOUTHFUL PRIVATE WHO LISTENED WITH EAGER EARS TO THE WORDS OF THE TALL SOLDIER AND THE VARIED COMMENTS OF HIS COMRADES.

AFTER RECEIVING A FILL OF DISCUSSIONS CONCERNING MARCHES AND ATTACKS, HE WENT TO HIS HUT.

HE WISHED TO BE ALONE WITH SOME THOUGHTS THAT HAD LATELY COME TO HIM.

HE LAY DOWN ON HIS BUNK. SO THEY WERE AT LAST GOING TO FIGHT. ON THE MORROW, PERHAPS, THEY WOULD BE A BATTLE, AND HE WOULD BE IN IT. HE COULD NOT ACCEPT WITH ASSURANCE AN OMEN THAT HE WAS ABOUT TO MINGLE IN ONE OF THOSE GREAT AFFAIRS OF THE EARTH.

HE HAD, OF COURSE, DREAMED OF BATTLES ALL HIS LIFE OF VAGUE AND BLOODY CONFLICTS THAT HAD THRILLED HIM WITH THEIR SWEEP AND FIRE... HE HAD REGARDED BATTLES AS CRIMSON BLOTCHES ON THE PAGES OF THE PAST. HE HAD PUT THEM AS THINGS OF THE BYGONE WITH HIS THOUGHT-IMAGES OF HEAVY CROWNS AND HIGH CASTLES.

FROM HIS HOME HIS YOUTHFUL EYES HAD LOOKED UPON THE WAR IN HIS OWN COUNTRY WITH DISTRUST. IT MUST BE SOME SORT OF PLAY AFFAIR, HE THOUGHT. HE HAD LONG DESPAIRED OF WITNESSING A GREEKLIKE STRUGGLE IN HIS OWN TIME... MEN WERE BETTER NOW, OR, AT LEAST MORE TIMID.

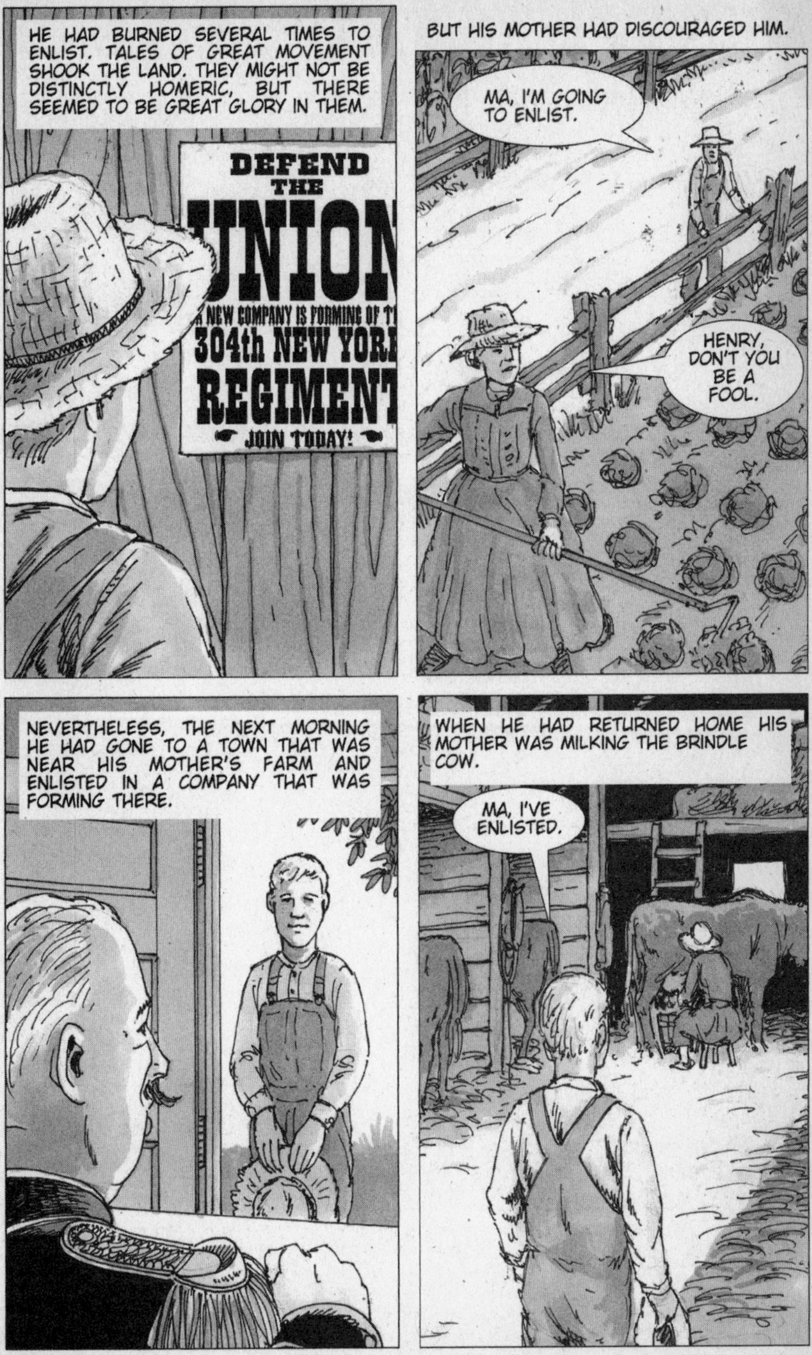
HE HAD BURNED SEVERAL TIMES TO ENLIST. TALES OF GREAT MOVEMENT SHOOK THE LAND. THEY MIGHT NOT BE DISTINCTLY HOMERIC, BUT THERE SEEMED TO BE GREAT GLORY IN THEM.
DEFEND THE UNION
NEW COMPANY IS FORMING OF T
304th NEW YOR
REGIMENT
JOIN TODAY!
BUT HIS MOTHER HAD DISCOURAGED HIM.
MA, I'M GOING TO ENLIST.
HENRY, DON'T YOU BE A FOOL.
NEVERTHELESS, THE NEXT MORNING HE HAD GONE TO A TOWN THAT WAS NEAR HIS MOTHER'S FARM AND ENLISTED IN A COMPANY THAT WAS FORMING THERE.
WHEN HE HAD RETURNED HOME HIS MOTHER WAS MILKING THE BRINDLE COW.
MA, I'VE ENLISTED.

THE LORD'S WILL BE DONE, HENRY.

WHEN HE HAD STOOD IN THE DOORWAY WITH HIS SOLDIER'S CLOTHES ON HIS BACK, HE HAD SEEN TWO TEARS LEAVING THEIR TRAILS ON HIS MOTHER'S SCARRED CHEEKS.

SHE HAD DISAPPOINTED HIM BY SAYING NOTHING WHATEVER ABOUT RETURNING WITH HIS SHIELD OR ON IT.

SHE THEN CONTINUED TO MILK THE BRINDLE COW.

HE HAD PREPARED CERTAIN SENTENCES WHICH HE THOUGHT COULD BE USED WITH TOUCHING EFFECT. BUT HER WORDS DESTROYED HIS PLANS.

YOU WATCH OUT, HENRY, AND TAKE GOOD CARE OF YOURSELF IN THIS FIGHTING BUSINESS. DON'T GO ATHINKIN' YOU CAN LICK THE HULL REBEL ARMY AT THE START, BECAUSE YEH CAN'T.

I'VE KNET YEH EIGHT PAIR OF SOCKS, HENRY, AND I'VE PUT IN ALL YER BEST SHIRTS, BECAUSE I WANT MY BOY TO BE JEST AS WARM AND COMFORTABLE AS ANYBODY IN THE ARMY.

AN' ALLUS BE CAREFUL AN CHOOSE YER COMPANY. THERE'S A LOT OF BAD MEN IN THE ARMY, HENRY. THE ARMY MAKES THEM WILD.

I DON'T WANT YEH TO EVER DO ANYTHING, HENRY, THAT YEH WOULD BE ASHAMED TO LET ME KNOW ABOUT.

YEH MUST ALLUS REMEMBER YER FATHER, TOO, CHILD, AN' REMEMBER HE NEVER DRUNK A DROP OF LICKER IN HIS LIFE, AND SELDOM SWORE A CROSS OATH.

I DON'T KNOW WHAT ELSE TO TELL YEH, HENRY, EXCEPTING THAT YEH MUST NEVER DO NO SHIRKING, CHILD, ON MY ACCOUNT. IF SO BE A TIME COMES WHEN YEH HAVE TO BE KILT OR DO A MEAN THING, WHY, HENRY, DON'T THINK OF ANYTHING EXCEPT WHAT'S RIGHT...

...BECAUSE THERE'S MANY A WOMAN HAS TO BEAR UP AGAINST SECH THINGS THESE TIMES, AND THE LORD WILL TAKE CARE OF US ALL.

WHEN HE LOOKED BACK FROM THE GATE, HE HAD SEEN HIS MOTHER KNEELING AMONG THE POTATO PARINGS. HER BROWN FACE, UPRAISED, WAS STAINED WITH TEARS, AND HER SPARE FORM WAS QUIVERING

HE BOWED HIS HEAD AND WENT ON, FEELING SUDDENLY ASHAMED OF HIS PURPOSE.

FROM HIS HOME HE HAD GONE TO THE SEMINARY TO BID ADIEU TO MANY SCHOOLMATES. THEY HAD THRONGED ABOUT HIM WITH WONDER AND ADMIRATION. HE FELT THE GULF NOW BETWEEN THEM AND HAD SWELLED WITH CALM PRIDE.

HE AND SOME OF HIS FELLOWS WHO HAD DONNED BLUE WERE QUITE OVERWHELMED WITH PRIVILEGES FOR ALL OF ONE AFTERNOON, AND IT HAD BEEN A VERY DELICIOUS THING...THEY HAD STRUTTED.

A CERTAIN LIGHT-HAIRED GIRL HAD MADE VIVACIOUS FUN AT HIS MARTIAL SPIRIT...

...BUT THERE WAS ANOTHER AND DARKER GIRL WHOM HE HAD GAZED AT STEADFASTLY, AND HE THOUGHT SHE GREW DEMURE AND SAD AT THE SIGHT OF HIS BLUE AND BRASS.

12

ON THE WAY TO WASHINGTON HIS SPIRIT HAD SOARED. THE REGIMENT WAS FED AND CARESED AT STATION AFTER STATION UNTIL THE YOUTH HAD BELIEVED THAT HE MUST BE A HERO.

AFTER COMPLICATED JOURNEYING WITH MANY PAUSES, THERE HAD COME MONTHS OF MONOTONOUS LIFE IN A CAMP. HE HAD HAD THE BELIEF THAT REAL WAR WAS A SERIES OF DEATH STRUGGLES WITH SMALL TIME IN BETWEEN FOR SLEEP AND MEALS;

BUT SINCE HIS REGIMENT HAD COME TO THE FIELD THE ARMY HAD DONE LITTLE BUT SIT STILL AND TRY TO KEEP WARM.

THE ONLY FOE HE HAD SEEN WERE SOME PICKETS ALONG THE RIVER BANK. THEY WERE A SUN-TANNED PHILOSOPHICAL LOT. HENRY, ON GUARD DUTY ONE NIGHT, CONVERSED ACROSS THE STREAM WITH ONE OF THEM. HE WAS A SLIGHTLY RAGGED MAN, WHO SPAT SKILLFULLY BETWEEN HIS SHOES AND POSSESSED A GREAT FUND OF BLAND AND INFANTILE ASSURANCE.

YANK, YER A RIGHT DUM *GOOD* FELLER.

THE YOUTH LIKED HIM PERSONALLY. THIS SENTIMENT, FLOATING TO HIM UPON THE STILL AIR, HAD MADE HIM TEMPORARILY REGRET WAR.

VARIOUS VETERANS HAD TOLD HIM TALES. SOME TALKED OF GRAY, BEWHISKERED HORDES WHO WERE ADVANCING WITH RELENTLESS CURSES AND CHEWING TOBACCO WITH UNSPEAKABLE VALOR.

THEY'LL CHARGE THROUGH HELL'S FIRE AN' BRIMSTONE T' GET A HOLD ON A HAVERSACK, AN' SECH STOMACHS AIN'T A-LASTIN' LONG.

STILL, HE COULD NOT PUT A WHOLE FAITH IN VETERANS' TALES, FOR RECRUITS WERE THEIR PREY.

14

HE PERCEIVED NOW THAT IT DID NOT GREATLY MATTER WHAT KIND OF SOLDIER HE WAS GOING TO FIGHT, SO LONG AS THEY FOUGHT, WHICH FACT NO ONE DISPUTED.

THERE WAS A MORE SERIOUS PROBLEM. HE LAY IN HIS BUNK PONDERING UPON IT. HE TRIED TO MATHEMATICALLY PROVE TO HIMSELF THAT HE WOULD NOT RUN FROM A BATTLE.

A LITTLE PANIC-FEAR GREW IN HIS MIND. AS HIS IMAGINATION WENT FORWARD TO A FIGHT, HE SAW HIDEOUS POSSIBILITIES.

THAT'S ALL RIGHT! YOU CAN BELIEVE ME OR NOT, JEST AS YOU LIKE.

PRETTY SOON YOU'LL FIND OUT 1 WAS RIGHT.

WELL, YOU DON'T KNOW EVERYTHING IN THE WORLD, DO YOU?

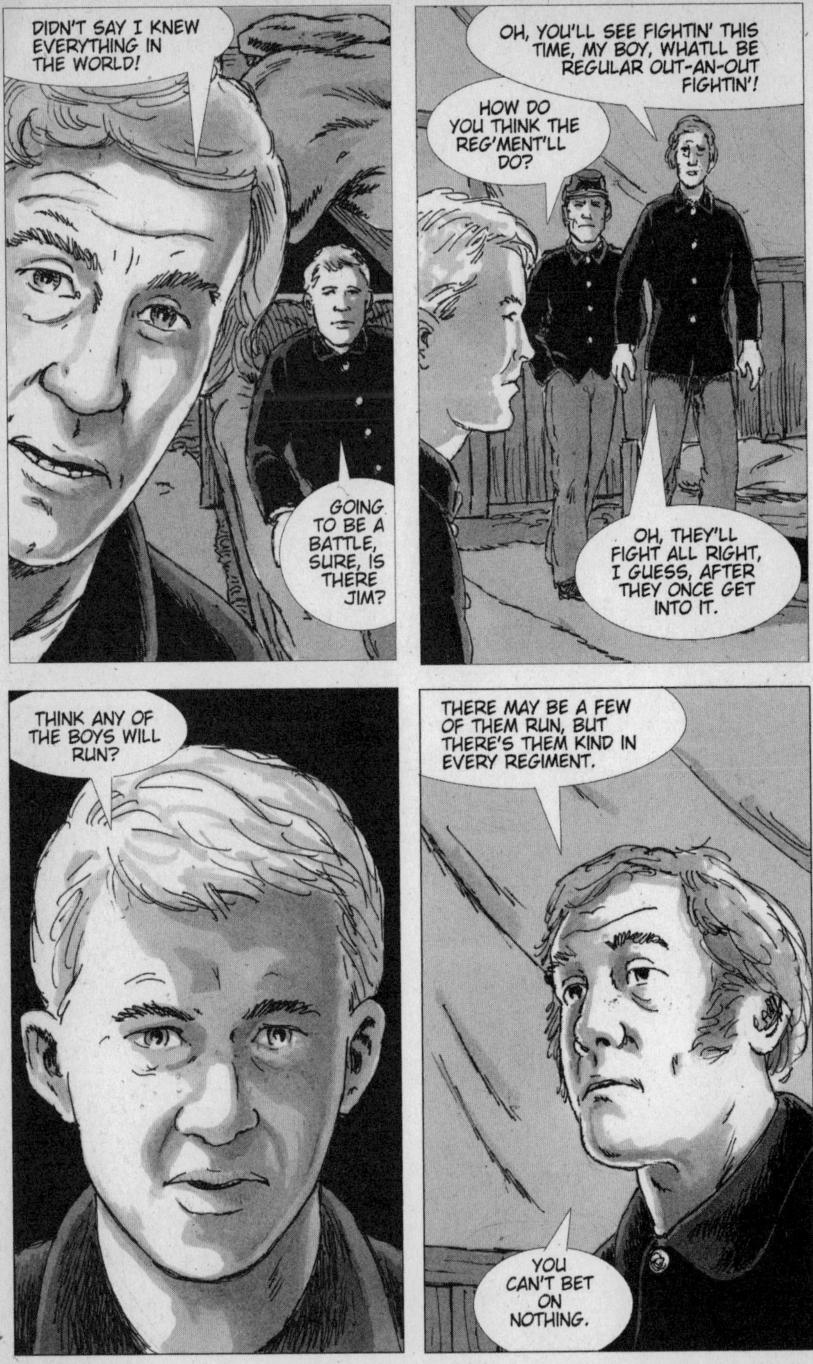
DIDN'T SAY I KNEW EVERYTHING IN THE WORLD!
GOING TO BE A BATTLE, SURE, IS THERE JIM?
OH, YOU'LL SEE FIGHTIN' THIS TIME, MY BOY, WHATLL BE REGULAR OUT-AN-OUT FIGHTIN'!
HOW DO YOU THINK THE REG'MENT'LL DO?
OH, THEY'LL FIGHT ALL RIGHT, I GUESS, AFTER THEY ONCE GET INTO IT.
THINK ANY OF THE BOYS WILL RUN?
THERE MAY BE A FEW OF THEM RUN, BUT THERE'S THEM KIND IN EVERY REGIMENT.
YOU CAN'T BET ON NOTHING.

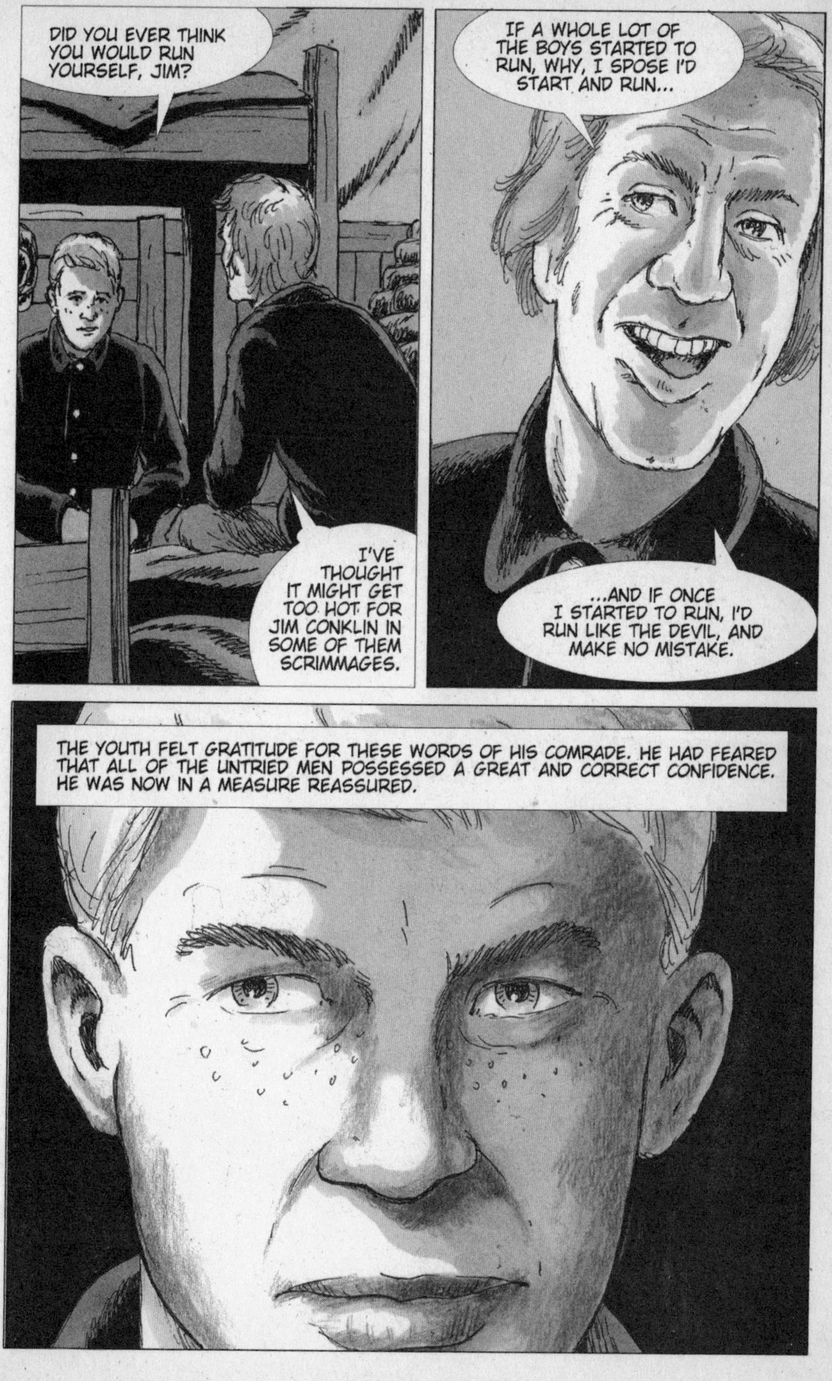
DID YOU EVER THINK YOU WOULD RUN YOURSELF, JIM?
I'VE THOUGHT IT MIGHT GET TOO HOT FOR JIM CONKLIN IN SOME OF THEM SCRIMMAGES.
IF A WHOLE LOT OF THE BOYS STARTED TO RUN, WHY, I SPOSE I'D START AND RUN...
...AND IF ONCE I STARTED TO RUN, I'D RUN LIKE THE DEVIL, AND MAKE NO MISTAKE.
THE YOUTH FELT GRATITUDE FOR THESE WORDS OF HIS COMRADE. HE HAD FEARED THAT ALL OF THE UNTRIED MEN POSSESSED A GREAT AND CORRECT CONFIDENCE. HE WAS NOW IN A MEASURE REASSURED.

EARLY ONE MORNING HE FOUND HIMSELF IN THE RANKS OF HIS PREPARED REGIMENT. THE MEN WERE WHISPERING SPECULATIONS AND RECOUNTING THE OLD RUMORS. IN THE GLOOM BEFORE THE BREAK OF DAY, THEIR UNIFORMS GLOWED A DEEP PURPLE HUE.

A MOMENT LATER THE REGIMENT WENT SWINGING OFF INTO THE DARKNESS. IT WAS NOW LIKE ONE OF THOSE MOVING MONSTERS WENDING WITH MANY FEET. THE AIR WAS HEAVY, AND COLD WITH DEW. A MASS OF WET GRASS, MARCHED UPON, RUSTLED LIKE SILK.

THE LONG SERPENTS CRAWLED SLOWLY FROM HILL TO HILL WITHOUT BLUSTER OF SMOKE. A DUNG-COLORED CLOUD OF DUST FLOATED AWAY TO THE RIGHT. THE SKY OVERHEAD WAS A FAIRY BLUE.

THE MEN BEGAN TO SPEAK OF VICTORY AS OF A THING THEY KNEW. ALSO. THE TALL SOLDIER RECEIVED HIS VINDICATION.

THE YOUTH, CONSIDERING HIMSELF AS SEPARATED FROM THE OTHERS, WAS SADDENED BY THE BLITHE AND MERRY SPEECHES THAT WENT FROM RANK TO RANK.

A RATHER FAT SOLDIER ATTEMPTED TO PILFER A HORSE FROM A DOORYARD, PLANNING TO LOAD HIS KNAPSACK UPON IT.

HE WAS ESCAPING WITH HIS PRIZE WHEN A YOUNG GIRL RUSHED FROM THE HOUSE AND GRABBED THE ANIMAL'S MANE.

THERE FOLLOWED A WRANGLE. THE YOUNG GIRL, WITH PINK CHEEKS AND SHINING EYES, STOOD LIKE A DAUNTLESS STATUE.

THE OBSERVANT REGIMENT, STANDING AT REST IN THE ROADWAY, WHOOPED AT ONCE, AND ENTERED WHOLE-SOULED UPON THE SIDE OF THE MAIDEN

HIT HIM WITH A STICK!

WHEN HE RETREATED WITHOUT THE HORSE, THE REGIMENT REJOICED.

21

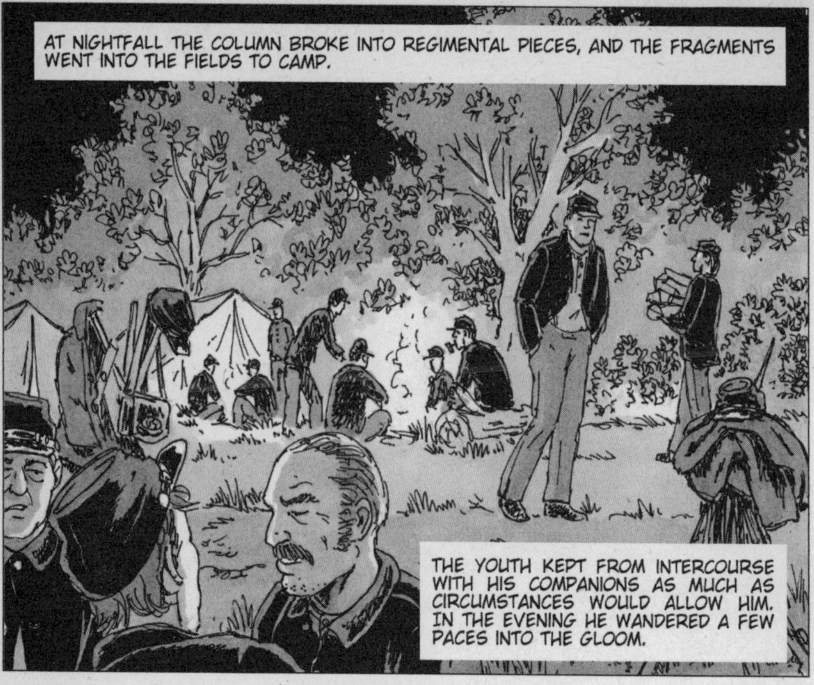
AT NIGHTFALL THE COLUMN BROKE INTO REGIMENTAL PIECES, AND THE FRAGMENTS WENT INTO THE FIELDS TO CAMP.
THE YOUTH KEPT FROM INTERCOURSE WITH HIS COMPANIONS AS MUCH AS CIRCUMSTANCES WOULD ALLOW HIM. IN THE EVENING HE WANDERED A FEW PACES INTO THE GLOOM.

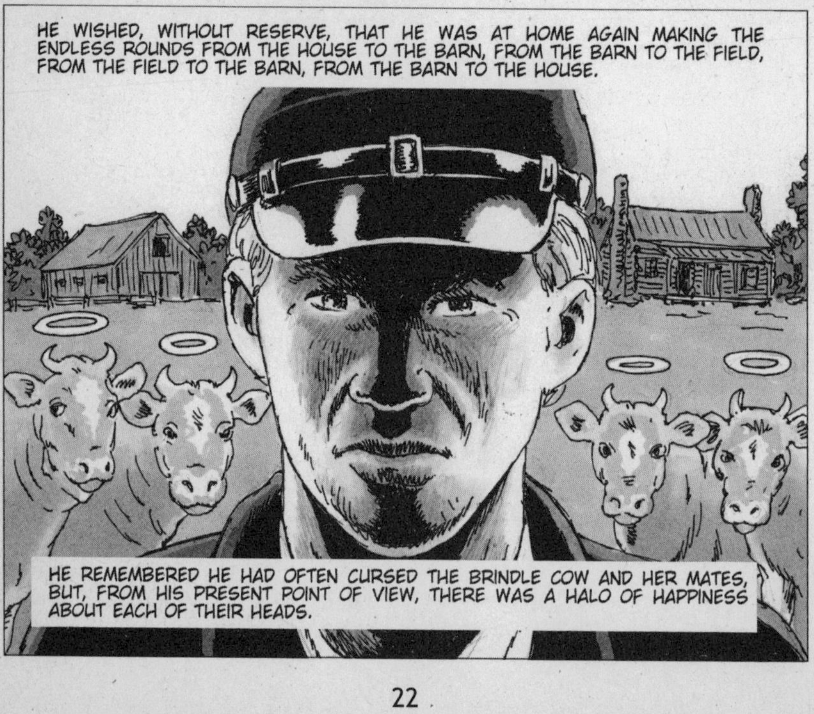
HE WISHED, WITHOUT RESERVE, THAT HE WAS AT HOME AGAIN MAKING THE ENDLESS ROUNDS FROM THE HOUSE TO THE BARN, FROM THE BARN TO THE FIELD, FROM THE FIELD TO THE BARN, FROM THE BARN TO THE HOUSE.
HE REMEMBERED HE HAD OFTEN CURSED THE BRINDLE COW AND HER MATES, BUT, FROM HIS PRESENT POINT OF VIEW, THERE WAS A HALO OF HAPPINESS ABOUT EACH OF THEIR HEADS.

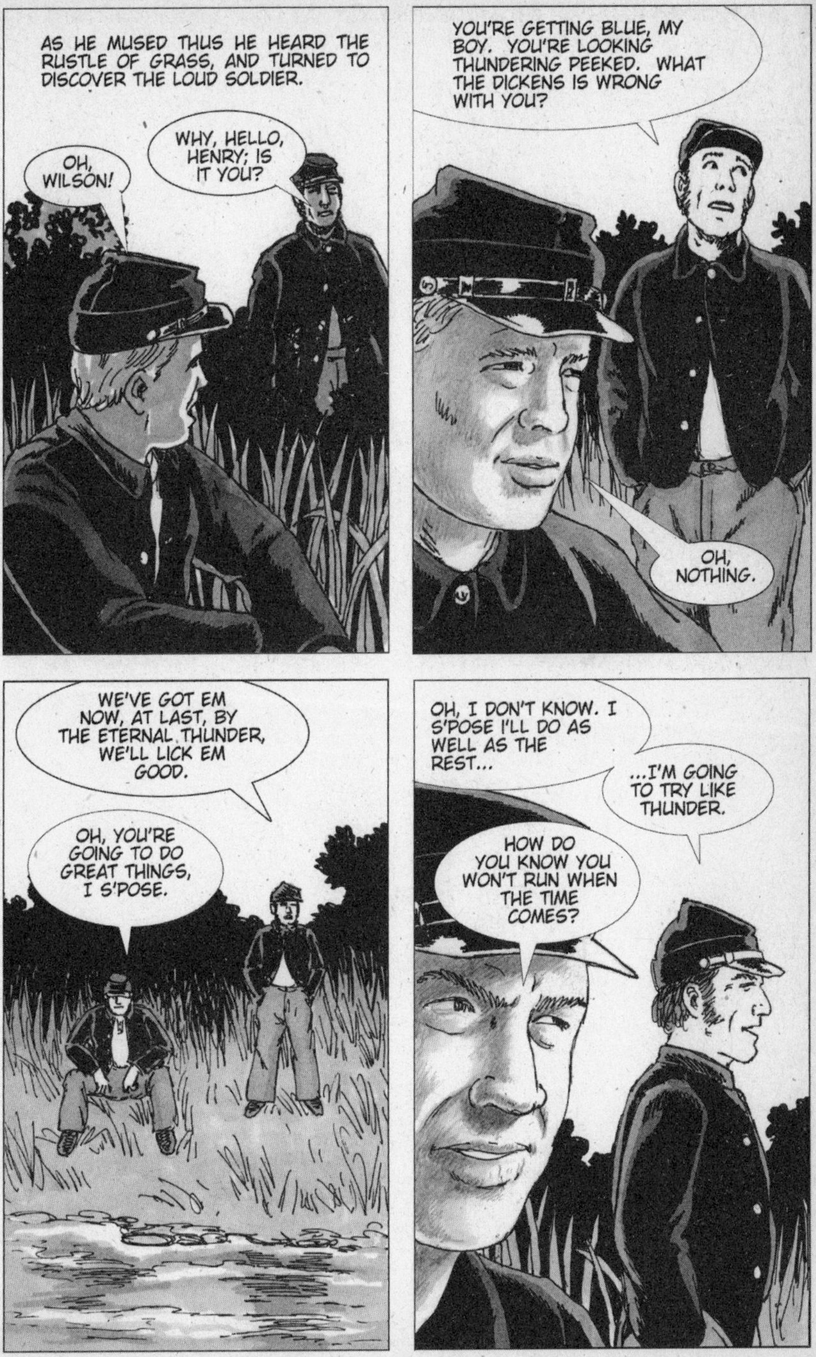
AS HE MUSED THUS HE HEARD THE RUSTLE OF GRASS, AND TURNED TO DISCOVER THE LOUD SOLDIER.
OH, WILSON!
WHY, HELLO, HENRY; IS IT YOU?
YOU'RE GETTING BLUE, MY BOY. YOU'RE LOOKING THUNDERING PEEKED. WHAT THE DICKENS IS WRONG WITH YOU?
OH, NOTHING.
WE'VE GOT EM NOW, AT LAST, BY THE ETERNAL THUNDER, WE'LL LICK EM GOOD.
OH, YOU'RE GOING TO DO GREAT THINGS, I S'POSE.
OH, I DON'T KNOW. I S'POSE I'LL DO AS WELL AS THE REST...
...I'M GOING TO TRY LIKE THUNDER.
HOW DO YOU KNOW YOU WON'T RUN WHEN THE TIME COMES?

RUN? RUN? OF COURSE NOT!

WELL, LOTS OF GOOD-A-ENOUGH MEN HAVE THOUGHT THEY WAS GOING TO DO GREAT THINGS BEFORE THE FIGHT, BUT WHEN THE TIME COME THEY SKEDADDLED.

YOU AIN'T THE BRAVEST MAN IN THE WORLD.

NO, I AIN'T! AND I DIDN'T SAY THAT I WAS! I SAID I WAS GOING TO DO MY SHARE OF THE FIGHTING!

YOU TALK AS IF YOU THOUGHT YOU WAS NAPOLEON BONAPARTE!

WELL, YOU NEEDN'T GIT MAD ABOUT IT!

HIS FAILURE TO DISCOVER ANY MITE OF RESEMBLANCE IN THEIR VIEW POINTS MADE HIM MORE MISERABLE THAN BEFORE.

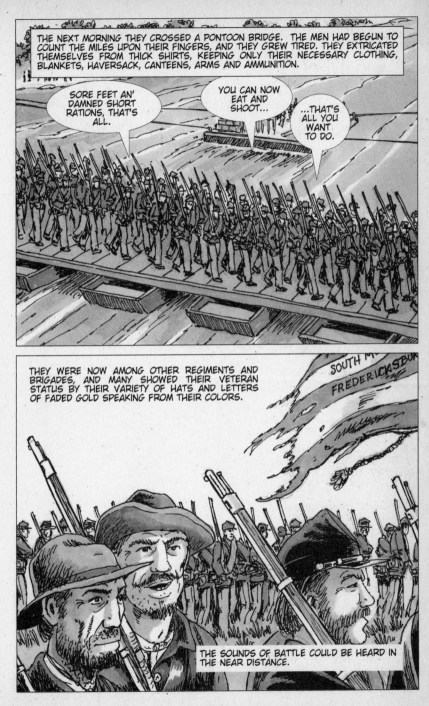

THE NEXT MORNING THEY CROSSED A PONTOON BRIDGE. THE MEN HAD BEGUN TO COUNT THE MILES UPON THEIR FINGERS, AND THEY GREW TIRED. THEY EXTRICATED THEMSELVES FROM THICK SHIRTS, KEEPING ONLY THEIR NECESSARY CLOTHING, BLANKETS, HAVERSACK, CANTEENS, ARMS AND AMMUNITION.

SORE FEET AN' DAMNED SHORT RATIONS, THAT'S ALL.

YOU CAN NOW EAT AND SHOOT...

...THAT'S ALL YOU WANT TO DO.

THEY WERE NOW AMONG OTHER REGIMENTS AND BRIGADES, AND MANY SHOWED THEIR VETERAN STATUS BY THEIR VARIETY OF HATS AND LETTERS OF FADED GOLD SPEAKING FROM THEIR COLORS.

SOUTH M...
FREDERICKSBURG

THE SOUNDS OF BATTLE COULD BE HEARD IN THE NEAR DISTANCE.

25

SUDDENLY THE ENTIRE REGIMENT FOUND THEMSELVES RUNNING DOWN A WOOD ROAD, THE MEN PANTING FROM THE FIRST EFFECTS OF SPEED. THE SUN SPREAD DISCLOSING RAYS, AND, ONE BY ONE, REGIMENTS BURST INTO VIEW LIKE ARMED MEN JUST BORN OF THE EARTH

SAY... WHAT'S ALL THIS... ABOUT?

WHAT TH' THUNDER WE SKEDADDLIN' THIS WAY FER?

THE YOUTH PERCEIVED THAT THE TIME HAD COME.

HE INSTANTLY SAW THAT IT WOULD BE IMPOSSIBLE FOR HIM TO ESCAPE FROM THE REGIMENT. IT INCLOSED HIM.

THE REGIMENT SLID DOWN A BANK AND WALLOWED ACROSS A LITTLE STREAM. AS THEY CLIMBED THE HILL ON THE FARTHER SIDE ARTILLERY BEGAN TO BOOM.

THERE WERE SOME LITTLE FIELDS GIRTED AND SQUEEZED BY A FOREST. SPREAD OVER THE GRASS AND IN AMONG THE TREE TRUNKS, HE COULD SEE KNOTS AND WAVING LINES OF SKIRMISHERS WHO WERE RUNNING HITHER AND THITHER AND FIRING AT THE LANDSCAPE. A DARK BATTLE LINE LAY UPON A SUNSTRUCK CLEARING THAT GLEAMED ORANGE COLOR. A FLAG FLUTTERED.

THE LINE ENCOUNTERED THE BODY OF A DEAD SOLDIER. HE LAY UPON HIS BACK STARING AT THE SKY .HE WAS DRESSED IN AN AWKWARD SUIT OF YELLOWISH BROWN.

THE YOUTH COULD SEE THAT THE SOLES OF HIS SHOES HAD BEEN WORN TO THE THINNESS OF WRITING PAPER. IT WAS AS IF FATE HAD BETRAYED THE SOLDIER,

IN DEATH IT EXPOSED TO HIS ENEMIES THAT POVERTY WHICH IN LIFE HE HAD PERHAPS CONCEALED FROM HIS FRIENDS.

ABSURD IDEAS TOOK HOLD UPON THE YOUTH. A HOUSE STANDING IN THE DISTANT FIELD HAD AN OMINOUS LOOK. THE SHADOWS OF THE WOODS WERE FORMIDABLE. HE WAS CERTAIN THAT IN THIS VISTA LURKED FIERCE EYED HOST.

THE SWIFT THOUGHT CAME TO HIM THAT THE GENERALS DID NOT KNOW WHAT THEY WERE ABOUT. IT WAS ALL A TRAP!

HE LOOKED AT THE MEN AROUND HIM, AND SAW, FOR THE MOST PART, EXPRESSIONS OF DEEP INTEREST, AS IF THEY WERE INVESTIGATING SOMETHING THAT HAD FASCINATED THEM. THE GREATER PART OF THE UNTESTED MEN APPEARED QUIET AND ABSORBED.

THEY WERE GOING TO LOOK AT WAR, THE RED ANIMAL WAR, THE BLOOD-SWOLLEN GOD.

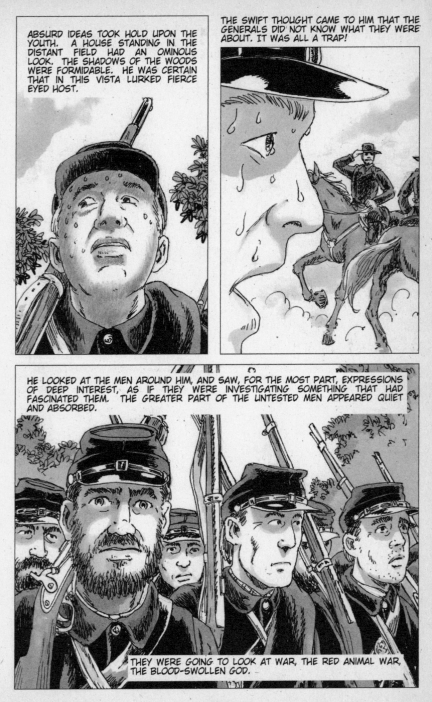

AFTER A TIME THE BRIGADE WAS HALTED IN THE CATHEDRAL LIGHT OF A FOREST. THE BUSY SKIRMISHERS WERE STILL POPPING. THROUGH THE AISLES OF THE WOODS COULD BE SEEN THE FLOATING SMOKE OF THEIR RIFLES.

DURING THE HALT MANY MEN IN THE REGIMENT BEGAN ERECTING TINY HILLS IN FRONT OF THEM. THEY USED STONES, STICKS, EARTH, AND ANYTHING THEY THOUGHT MIGHT TURN A BULLET.

THIS PROCEDURE CAUSED A DISCUSSION AMONG THE MEN. SOME WISHED TO FIGHT LIKE DUELISTS, BELIEVING IT TO BE CORRECT TO STAND ERECT.

OTHERS SCOFFED IN REPLY, AND POINTED TO THE VETERANS ON THE FLANKS WHO WERE DIGGING AT THE GROUND LIKE TERRIERS.

DIRECTLY, HOWEVER, THEY WERE ORDERED TO WITHDRAW FROM THAT PLACE.

THEY WERE MOVED TO ANOTHER PLACE. THEY ATE THEIR NOON MEAL BEHIND A THIRD ONE. THEY WERE MARCHED FROM PLACE TO PLACE WITH APPARENT AIMLESSNESS.

WELL, THEN WHAT DID THEY MARCH US OUT HERE FOR?

I DON'T SEE WHAT GOOD IT DOES TO WEAR OUT OUR LEGS FOR NOTHIN'.

NEITHER DO I!

IT AIN'T RIGHT! I TELL YOU THAT IF ANYBODY WITH ANY SENSE WAS-A-RUNNING THIS ARMY IT...

THE TALL PRIVATE HAD HEARD ENOUGH...

OH, SHUT UP!

YOU LITTLE FOOL. YOU DAMNED LITTLE CUSS! YOU AIN'T HAD THAT COAT ON FOR SIX MONTHS, AND YET YOU TALK AS IF...

WELL, I WANTA DO SOME FIGHTIN' ANYWAY...

THAT AFTERNOON THE REGIMENT WENT OVER THE SAME GROUND IT HAD TAKEN IN THE MORNING. WHEN THEY BEGAN TO PASS INTO A NEW REGION. HIS OLD FEARS OF STUPIDITY AND INCOMPETENCE REASSAILED HIM.

THE SKIRMISH FIRE INCREASED TO A LONG CHATTERING SOUND. WITH IT WAS MINGLED FAR AWAY CHEERING. A BATTERY SPOKE.

DIRECTLY THE YOUTH WOULD SEE THE SKIRMISHERS RUNNING. THEY WERE PURSUED BY THE SOUND OF MUSKETRY FIRE. AFTER A TIME THE HOT, DANGEROUS FLASHED OF THE RIFLES WERE VISIBLE.

THE DIN BECAME A CRESCENDO, LIKE THE ROAR OF AN ONCOMING TRAIN.

SUDDENLY, THE YOUTH FELT A HEAVY AND SAD HAND LAID ON HIS SHOULDER.

IT'S MY FIRST AND LAST BATTLE, OLD BOY.

EH?

I'M A GONE COON THIS TIME AND AND I W-WANT YOU TO TAKE THESE THINGS TO MY FOLKS.

WHY, WHAT THE DEVIL?

THE LOUD SOLDIER GAVE HIM A GLANCE AS FROM THE DEPTHS OF A TOMB.

THE BRIGADE WAS HALTED IN THE FRINGE OF A GROVE. BULLETS BEGAN TO WHISTLE AMONG THE BRANCHES AND NIP AT THE TREES. TWIGS AND LEAVES CAME SAILING DOWN.

THE LIEUTENANT OF THE YOUTH'S COMPANY WAS SHOT IN THE HAND. HE BEGAN TO SWEAR WONDROUSLY, AS IF HE HAD HIT HIS FINGER WITH A TACK HAMMER AT HOME.

A NERVOUS LAUGHTER WENT ALONG THE REGIMENTAL LINE, RELIEVING THE TIGHTENED SENSES OF THE NEW MEN.

THE BATTLE FLAGS IN THE DISTANCE JERKED ABOUT MADLY. THEY SEEMED TO BE STRUGGLING TO FREE THEMSELVES FROM AN AGONY.

MEN RUNNING SWIFTLY EMERGED FROM THE SMOKE. THEY GREW IN NUMBER UNTIL IT WAS SEEN THAT THE WHOLE COMMAND WAS FLEEING

THE VETERAN REGIMENTS ON THE RIGHT AND LEFT BEGAN TO JEER. AT THE FLEEING MEN. WITH THE PASSIONATE SONG OF THE BULLETS AND THE BANSHEE SHRIEKS OF SHELLS WERE MINGLED LOUD CATCALLS AND BITS OF FACETIOUS ADVICE CONCERNING PLACES OF SAFETY.

OVER THIS TUMULT COULD BE HEARD THE GRIM JOKES OF THE CRITICAL VETERANS; BUT THE RETREATING MEN APPARENTLY WERE NOT EVEN CONSCIOUS OF THE PRESENCE OF AN AUDIENCE.

THE COMPOSITE MONSTER WHICH HAD CAUSED THE OTHERS TO FLEE HAD NOT THEN APPEARED. THE YOUTH RESOLVED TO GET A VIEW OF IT, AND THEN, HE THOUGHT HE MIGHT LIKELY RUN BETTER THAN THE BEST OF THEM.

THEN SOMEONE CRIED

HERE THEY COME!

ACROSS THE SMOKE-INFESTED FIELDS CAME A BROWN SWARM OF RUNNING MEN WHO WERE GIVING SHRILL YELLS. THEY CAME ON, STOOPING AND SWINGING THEIR RIFLES AT ALL ANGLES.

A FLAG, TILTED FORWARD, SPED NEAR THE FRONT.

A HATLESS GENERAL PULLED HIS DRIPPING HORSE TO A STAND HEAR THE COLONEL OF THE 304TH.

THE CAPTAIN OF THE COMPANY HAD BEEN PACING EXCITEDLY TO AND FRO. HE COAXED IN SCHOOLMISTRESS FASHION, AS TO A CONGREGATION OF BOYS WITH PRIMERS.

PERSPIRATION STREAMED DOWN THE YOUTH'S FACE, WHICH WAS SOILED LIKE THAT OF A WEEPING URCHIN. HE FREQUENTLY, WITH A NERVOUS MOVEMENT, WIPED HIS EYES WITH HIS COAT SLEEVE.

HE GOT ONE GLANCE AT THE FOE-SWARMING FIELD IN FRONT OF HIM, AND INSTANTLY CEASED TO DEBATE THE QUESTION OF HIS PIECE BEING LOADED.

BEFORE HE WAS READY TO BEGIN, BEFORE HE HAD ANNOUNCED TO HIMSELF THAT HE WAS ABOUT TO FIGHT, HE THREW THE OBEDIENT, WELL-BALANCED RIFLE INTO POSITION AND...

HE SUDDENLY LOST CONCERN FOR HIMSELF, AND FORGOT TO LOOK AT A MENACING FATE. HE BECAME NOT A MAN BUT A MEMBER.

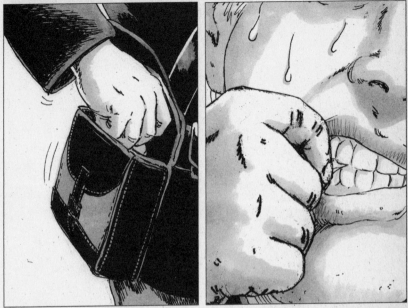

HE FELT THAT SOMETHING OF WHICH HE WAS A PART — A REGIMENT, AN ARMY, A CAUSE, OR A COUNTRY — WAS IN CRISIS. HE WAS WELDED INTO A COMMON PERSONALITY WHICH WAS DOMINATED BY A SINGLE DESIRE.

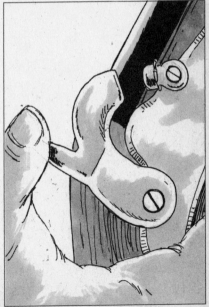

41

FOR SOME MOMENTS HE COULD NOT FLEE NO MORE THAN A LITTLE FINGER CAN COMMIT A REVOLUTION FROM A HAND.

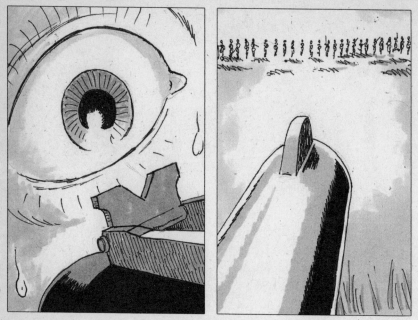

THE LIEUTENANT OF THE YOUTH'S COMPANY HAD ENCOUNTERED A SOLDIER WHO HAD FLED SCREAMING AT THE FIRST VOLLEY OF HIS COMRADES.

THE MAN WAS BLUBBERING AND STARING WITH SHEEPLIKE EYES AT THE LIEUTENANT, WHO HAD SEIZED HIM BY THE COLLAR AND WAS POMMELING HIM. HE DROVE HIM BACK INTO THE RANKS WITH MANY BLOWS

THE SOLDIER TRIED TO RELOAD HIS GUN, BUT HIS SHAKING HANDS PREVENTED. THE LIEUTENANT WAS OBLIGED TO ASSIST HIM.

THE MEN DROPPED HERE AND THERE LIKE BUNDLES.

THE CAPTAIN OF THE YOUTH'S COMPANY HAD BEEN KILLED, HIS BODY STRETCHED OUT IN THE POSITION OF A TIRED MAN RESTING.

ANOTHER GRUNTED SUDDENLY AS IF HE HAD BEEN STRUCK BY A CLUB IN THE STOMACH. HE SAT DOWN AND GAZED RUEFULLY.

FARTHER UP THE LINE A MAN, STANDING BEHIND A TREE, HAD HIS KNEE JOINT SPLINTERED BY A BALL. THERE HE REMAINED, CLINGING DESPERATELY TO THE TREE, AND CRYING FOR ASSISTANCE.

AT LAST AN EXULTANT YELL WENT ALONG THE QUIVERING LINE. THE FIRING DWINDLED FROM AN UPROAR TO A LAST VINDICTIVE POPPING.

AS THE SMOKE SLOWLY EDDIED AWAY, THE YOUTH SAW THAT THE CHARGE HAD BEEN REPULSED. THE ENEMY WERE SCATTERED INTO RELUCTANT GROUPS.

SOME OF THE REGIMENT BEGAN TO WHOOP FRENZIEDLY. MANY WERE SILENT. APPARENTLY THEY WERE TRYING TO CONTEMPLATE THEMSELVES.

AFTER THE FEVER HAD LEFT HIS VEINS, THE YOUTH BECAME AWARE OF THE FOUL ATMOSPHERE IN WHICH HE HAD BEEN STRUGGLING.

HE WAS GRIMY AND DRIPPING LIKE A LABORER IN A FOUNDRY.

A SENTENCE WITH VARIATIONS WENT UP AND DOWN THE LINE.

WELL, WE HELT EM BACK. WE HELT EM BACK.

DERNED IF WE HAVEN'T.

THE MEN SAID IT BLISSFULLY, LEERING AT EACH OTHER WITH DIRTY SMILES.

UNDER FOOT WERE A FEW GHASTLY FORMS MOTIONLESS. THEY LAY TWISTED IN FANTASTIC CONTORTIONS.

THEY LOOKED TO BE DUMPED OUT UPON THE GROUND FROM THE SKY.

THE YOUTH AWAKENED SLOWLY. SO IT WAS ALL OVER AT LAST! THE SUPREME TRIAL HAD BEEN PASSED. THE RED, FORMIDABLE DIFFICULTIES OF WAR HAD BEEN VANQUISHED.

HE HAD THE MOST DELIGHTFUL SENSATIONS OF HIS LIFE. STANDING AS IF APART FROM HIMSELF, HE VIEWED THAT LAST SCENE. HE PERCEIVED THAT THE MAN WHO HAD FOUGHT THUS WAS MAGNIFICENT.

HE FELT LIKE HE WAS A FINE FELLOW. HE SAW HIMSELF EVEN WITH THOSE IDEALS WHICH HE HAD CONSIDERED BEYOND HIM. HE SMILED IN DEEP GRATIFICATION.

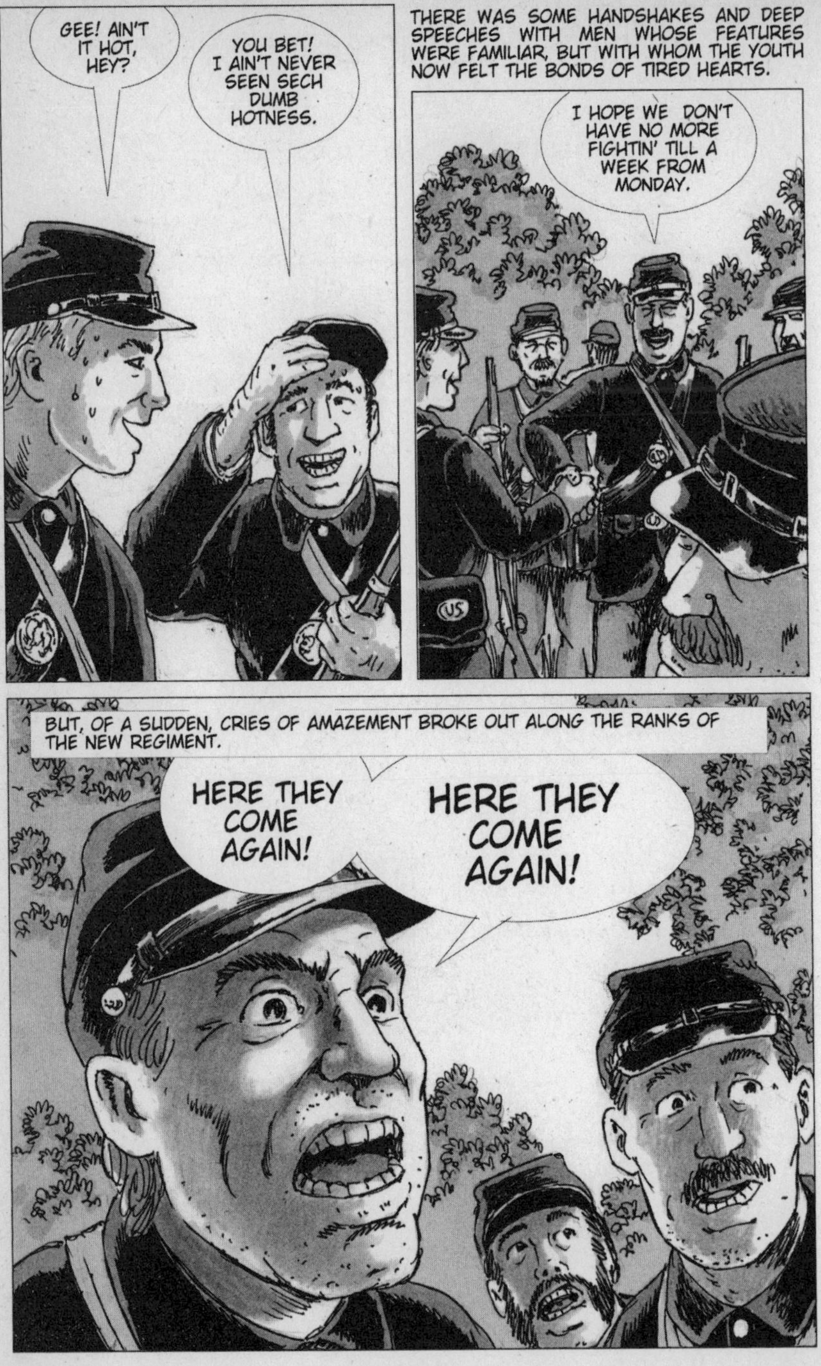
GEE! AIN'T IT HOT, HEY?
YOU BET! I AIN'T NEVER SEEN SECH DUMB HOTNESS.
THERE WAS SOME HANDSHAKES AND DEEP SPEECHES WITH MEN WHOSE FEATURES WERE FAMILIAR, BUT WITH WHOM THE YOUTH NOW FELT THE BONDS OF TIRED HEARTS.
I HOPE WE DON'T HAVE NO MORE FIGHTIN' TILL A WEEK FROM MONDAY.
BUT, OF A SUDDEN, CRIES OF AMAZEMENT BROKE OUT ALONG THE RANKS OF THE NEW REGIMENT.
HERE THEY COME AGAIN!
HERE THEY COME AGAIN!

THE YOUTH TURNED QUICK EYES UPON THE FIELD. HE DISCERNED FORMS BEGIN TO SWELL IN MASSES OUT OF A DISTANT WOOD. HE AGAIN SAW THE TILTED FLAG SPEEDING FORWARD.

THE MEN GROANED. THE LUSTER FADED FROM THEIR EYES. THEIR SMUDGED COUNTENANCES NOW EXPRESSED A PROFOUND DEJECTION.

THE YOUTH STARED. SURELY, HE THOUGHT, THIS IMPOSSIBLE THING WAS NOT ABOUT TO HAPPEN. HE WAITED AS IF HE EXPECTED THE ENEMY TO SUDDENLY STOP, APOLOGIZE, AND RETIRE BOWING. IT WAS ALL A MISTAKE.

OH, SAY, THIS IS TOO MUCH OF A GOOD THING...

...WHY CAN'T SOMEBODY SEND US SUPPORTERS?

TO THE YOUTH IT WAS AN ONSLAUGHT OF REDOUBTABLE DRAGONS. HE BECAME LIKE THE MAN WHO LOST HIS LEGS AT THE APPROACH OF THE RED AND GREEN MONSTER.

A MAN NEAR HIM WHO UP TO THIS TIME HAD BEEN WORKING FEVERISHLY AT HIS RIFLE SUDDENLY STOPPED AND RAN WITH HOWLS.

A LAD WHOSE FACE HAD BORNE AN EXPRESSION OF EXALTED COURAGE, THREW DOWN HIS GUN AND FLED. THERE WAS A REVELATION. THERE WAS NO SHAME ON HIS FACE.

HE RAN LIKE A RABBIT.

OTHERS BEGAN TO SCAMPER AWAY THROUGH THE SMOKE. HE SAW THE FEW FLEETING FORMS.

HE YELLED THEN WITH FRIGHT AND SWUNG ABOUT.

FOR A MOMENT, HE LOST THE DIRECTION OF SAFETY. DESTRUCTION THREATENED HIM FROM ALL POINTS.

DIRECTLY HE BEGAN TO SPEED TOWARD THE REAR IN GREAT LEAPS. HIS RIFLE AND CAP WERE GONE. HIS UNBUTTONED COAT BULGED IN THE WIND. THE FLAP OF HIS CARTRIDGE BOX BOBBED WILDLY, AND HIS CANTEEN, BY ITS SLENDER CORD, SWUNG OUT BEHIND.

HE RAN LIKE A BLIND MAN. TWO OR THREE TIMES HE FELL DOWN. ONCE HE KNOCKED HIS SHOULDER SO HEAVILY AGAINST A TREE THAT HE WENT HEADLONG.

SINCE HE HAD TURNED HIS BACK UPON THE FIGHT HIS FEARS HAD BEEN WONDROUSLY MAGNIFIED. DEATH ABOUT TO THRUST HIM BETWEEN THE SHOULDER BLADES WAS FAR MORE DREADFUL THAN DEATH ABOUT TO SMITE HIM BETWEEN THE EYES.

AS HE RAN HE MINGLED WITH OTHERS. IN HIS FLIGHT THE SOUND OF THESE FOLLOWING FOOTSTEPS GAVE HIM ONE MEAGER RELIEF.

HE EXPERIENCED A THRILL OF AMAZEMENT WHEN HE CAME WITHIN VIEW OF A BATTERY IN ACTION. THE MEN THERE SEEMED TO BE IN CONVENTIONAL MOODS, ALTOGETHER UNAWARE OF THE IMPENDING ANNIHILATION.

THE YOUTH PITIED THEM AS HE RAN. METHODICAL IDIOTS! MACHINE-LIKE FOOLS! THE REFINED JOY OF PLANTING SHELLS IN THE MIDST OF THE OTHER BATTERY'S FORMATION WOULD APPEAR A LITTLE THING WHEN THE INFANTRY CAME SWOOPING OUT OF THE WOODS.

THE YOUTH WENT ON, MODERATING HIS PACE SINCE HE HAD LEFT THE PLACE OF NOISES. HE CAME UPON A GENERAL OF DIVISION SEATED UPON A HORSE THAT PRICKED ITS EARS IN AN INTERESTED WAY AT THE BATTLE. HE WENT AS NEAR AS HE DARED TRYING TO OVERHEAR WORDS. OTHER MOUNTED MEN CIRCLED AROUND HIM.

TOMPKINS, GO OVER AN' SEE TAYLOR, AN' TELL HIM NOT TO BE IN SUCH AN ALL-FIRED HURRY...

SAY I THINK TH' CENTER WILL BREAK IF WE DON'T HELP IT OUT SOME.

A MOMENT LATER THE YOUTH SAW THE GENERAL BOUNCE EXCITEDLY IN THE SADDLE FROM SOME INFORMATION HE HAD JUST RECEIVED.

YES, BY HEAVENS, THEY HAVE...

YES, BY HEAVENS, THEY'VE HELD EM! THEY'VE HELD EM!

THE YOUTH CRINGED AS IF DISCOVERED IN A CRIME. BY HEAVENS, THEY HAD WON AFTER ALL! THE IMBECILE LINE HAD REMAINED AND BECOME VICTORS.

HE COULD HEAR CHEERING.

HE TURNED AWAY AMAZED AND ANGRY. HE FELT THAT HE HAD BEEN WRONGED.

THOUGHTS OF HIS COMRADES CAME TO HIM. THE BRITTLE BLUE LINE HAD WITHSTOOD THE BLOWS AND WON. HE GREW BITTER OVER IT. IT SEEMED THAT THE BLIND IGNORANCE AND STUPIDITY OF THESE LITTLE PIECES HAD BETRAYED HIM.

HE WONDERED WHAT THEY WOULD REMARK WHEN LATER HE APPEARED IN CAMP. HIS MIND HEARD HOWLS OF DERISION. THEIR DENSITY WOULD NOT ENABLE THEM TO UNDERSTAND HIS SHARPER POINT OF VIEW.

HE WENT FROM THE FIELD INTO A THICK WOOD, AS IF RESOLVED TO BURY HIMSELF. HE WISHED TO GET OUT OF THE HEARING OF THE CRACKING SHOTS WHICH WERE TO HIM LIKE VOICES.

THE GROUND WAS CLUTTERED WITH VINES AND BUSHES, AND THE TREES GREW CLOSE AND SPREAD OUT LIKE BOUQUETS. HE WAS OBLIGED TO FORCE HIS WAY WITH MUCH NOISE.

HE THREW A PINE CONE AT A JOVIAL SQUIRREL, AND HE WATCHED IT RUN AWAY WITH CHATTERING.

THE YOUTH FELT TRIUMPHANT AT THIS EXHIBITION. NATURE HAD GIVEN HIM A SIGN...

AT LENGTH HE REACHED A PLACE WHERE THE HIGH, ARCHING BOUGHS MADE A CHAPEL. PINE NEEDLES WERE A GENTLE BROWN CARPET. THERE WAS A RELIGIOUS HALF-LIGHT.

NEAR THE THRESHOLD HE STOPPED, HORROR-STRICKEN AT THE SIGHT OF THE THING.

HE WAS BEING LOOKED AT BY A DEAD MAN WHO WAS SEATED WITH HIS BACK AGAINST A TREE. THE CORPSE WAS DRESSED IN A UNIFORM THAT ONCE HAD BEEN BLUE, BUT WAS NOW FADED TO A MELANCHOLY SHADE OF GREEN.

OVER THE GRAY SKIN OF THE FACE RAN LITTLE ANTS,

THE YOUTH GRADUALLY BEGAN TO BACK AWAY FROM THE THING, ALL THE TIME FACING HIM. HE FEARED THAT IF HE TURNED HIS BACK THE BODY MIGHT SPRING UP AND STEALTHILY PURSUE HIM.

WHEN THE TREES BEGAN SOFTLY TO SING A HYMN OF TWILIGHT, THE YOUTH SUDDENLY STOPPED. THERE SUDDENLY BROKE A TREMENDOUS CLANGOR OF SOUNDS.

HE BEGAN TO RUN IN THE DIRECTION OF THE BATTLE. HE SAW THAT IT WAS AN IRONICAL THING FOR HIM TO BE RUNNING THUS TOWARD THAT WHICH HE HAD BEEN AT SUCH PAINS TO AVOID.

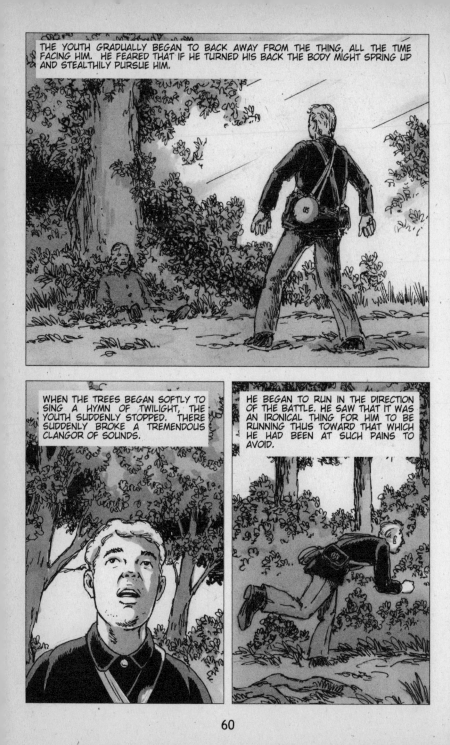

PRESENTLY HE WAS WHERE HE COULD SEE LONG GRAY WALLS OF VAPOR WHERE LAY BATTLE LINES. THE VOICES OF CANNON SHOOK HIM. THE MUSKETRY SOUNDED IN LONG IRRUGULAR SURGES THAT PLAYED HAVOC WITH HIS EARS. HE STOOD REGARDANT FOR A MOMENT. HIS EYES HAD AN AWESTRUCK EXPRESSION. HE GAWKED IN THE DIRECTION OF THE FIGHT.

HE CAME TO A FENCE AND CLAMBERED OVER IT. ON THE FAR SIDE, THE GROUND WAS LITTERED WITH CLOTHES AND GUNS. FOUR OR FIVE CORPSES KEPT MORNFUL COMPANY.

A HOT SUN HAD BLAZED UPON THE SPOT.

IN THIS PLACE THE YOUTH FELT THAT HE WAS AN INVADER. THIS FORGOTTEN PART OF THE BATTLE GROUND WAS OWNED BY THE DEAD MEN, AND HE HURRIED AWAY BEFORE ONE OF THE SWOLLEN FORMS WOULD TELL HIM TO BE BEGONE.

HE FINALLY CAME TO A LANE WHERE A BLOOD-STAINED CROWD STREAMED TOWARD THE REAR. THE WOUNDED MEN WERE CURSING, GROANING, AND WAILING.

ONE WAS MARCHING WITH THE AIR IMITATIVE OF SOME SUBLIME DRUM MAJOR. UPON HIS FEATURES WAS AN UNHOLY MIXTURE OF MERRIMENT AND AGONY. AS HE MARCHED HE SANG A BIT OF DOGGEREL IN A HIGH AND QUAVERING VOICE:

SING A SONG AH VIC'TRY,
A POCKET FULL AH BULLETS,
FIVE AN' TWENTY DEAD MEN
BAKED IN A PIE.

SOME ALREADY HAD THE GRAY SEAL OF DEATH UPON THEIR FACES: LIPS CURLED IN HARD LINES AT TEETH CLENCHED. OTHERS PROCEEDED SULLENLY, FULL OF ANGER AND THEIR WOUNDS, AND READY TO TURN UPON ANYTHING AS AN OBSCURE CAUSE.

THE YOUTH JOINED THIS CROWD AND MARCHED ALONG WITH IT. THE TORN BODIES EXPRESSED THE AWFUL MACHINERY IN WHICH THE MEN HAD BEEN ENTANGLED.

THERE WAS A TATTERED MAN, FOULED WITH DUST, BLOOD AND POWDER STAIN FROM HAIR TO SHOES, WHO TRUDGED QUIETLY AT THE YOUTH'S SIDE.

WAS PRETTY GOOD FIGHT, WA'N'T IT?

WHAT?

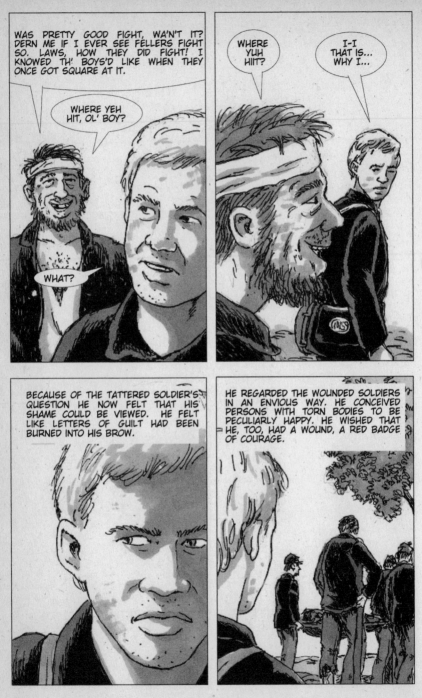

WAS PRETTY GOOD FIGHT, WA'N'T IT? DERN ME IF I EVER SEE FELLERS FIGHT SO. LAWS, HOW THEY DID FIGHT! I KNOWED TH' BOYS'D LIKE WHEN THEY ONCE GOT SQUARE AT IT.

WHERE YEH HIT, OL' BOY?

WHAT?

WHERE YUH HIIT?

I—I THAT IS... WHY I...

BECAUSE OF THE TATTERED SOLDIER'S QUESTION HE NOW FELT THAT HIS SHAME COULD BE VIEWED. HE FELT LIKE LETTERS OF GUILT HAD BEEN BURNED INTO HIS BROW.

HE REGARDED THE WOUNDED SOLDIERS IN AN ENVIOUS WAY. HE CONCEIVED PERSONS WITH TORN BODIES TO BE PECULIARLY HAPPY. HE WISHED THAT HE, TOO, HAD A WOUND, A RED BADGE OF COURAGE.

SUDDENLY THE GESTURE OF A MAN AHEAD OF HIM MADE THE YOUTH START AS IF BITTEN. THE MAN TURNED HIS WAXLIKE FEATURES TOWARD HIM.

GAWD! JIM CONKLIN!

HELLO, HENRY.

OH, JIM... OH, JIM, OH, JIM...

YEH KNOW, I WAS OUT THERE. AN, LORD, WHAT A CIRCUS! AN', B'JIMINEY, I GOT SHOT. I GOT SHOT.

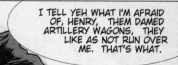

I TELL YEH WHAT I'M AFRAID OF, HENRY, THEM DAMED ARTILLERY WAGONS, THEY LIKE AS NOT RUN OVER ME. THAT'S WHAT.

I'LL TAKE CARE OF YEH, JIM. I SWEAR T' GAWD I WILL!

BUT THE TALL SOLDIER CONTINUED TO BE IN A LOWLY WAY. HE HUNG BABE LIKE TO THE YOUTH'S ARM. HIS EYES ROLLED IN THE WILDNESS OF HIS TERROR.

THE TALL SOLDIER SUDDENLY SEEMED TO FORGET ALL HIS FEARS. HE BECAME AGAIN THE GRIM, STALKING SPECTER OF A SOLDIER. HE PUSHED THE YOUTH AWAY.

I WAS ALLUS A GOOD FRIEND T' YEH, WA'N'T I, HENRY? I'VE ALLUS BEEN A PRETTY GOOD FELLA?

NO, NO, NO, LEAVE ME BE. LEAVE ME BE...

THE TALL SOLDIER WENT STAGGERING THROUGH THE GRASS BESIDE THE ROAD. THE YOUTH AND THE TATTERED MAN FOLLOWED CLOSELY.

LEAVE ME BE, LEAVE ME BE...

GAWD! HE'S RUNNIN'!

WHERE YEH GOIN', JIM? WHAT'S THE MATTER WITH YOU? TELL ME, WON'T YOU, JIM.

LEAVE ME BE, CAN'T YEH? LEAVE ME BE FER JUST A MINUTE.

THE YOUTH AND THE TATTERED MAN HUNG BACK BUT CONTINUED TO FOLLOW AS THE TALL SOLDIER STUMBLED ACROSS THE GRASSY FIELD

THE TALL SOLDIER STOPPED, AS IF HE HAD FOUND THE SPOT HE WAS LOOKING FOR... HE STOOD MOTIONLESS FOR A MOMENT. THEN HIS FORM STIFFENED AND STRAIGHTENED.

THERE WAS A SLIGHT RENDING SOUND. THEN HE BEGAN TO SWING FORWARD, FALLING LIKE A GIANT TREE.

THE YOUTH ROLLED TO HIS FRIEND AND ROLLED HIM OVER. HIS BLUE COAT FLAP FELL OPEN. HIS SIDE LOOKED AS IF IT HAD BEEN CHEWED BY WOLVES.

WELL, HE WAS A REG'LAR JIM-DANDY FOR NERVE WA'N'T HE?

I WONDER WHERE HE GOT HIS STREN'TH FROM?

THE YOUTH DESIRED TO SCREECH OUT HIS GRIEF, BUT HIS TONGUE LAY DEAD IN THE TOMB OF HIS MOUTH.

LOOK-A-HERE, PARDNER. HE'S UP AN' GONE, AIN'T HE?

WE MIGHT AS WELL BEGIN T' LOOK AFTER OL' NUMBER ONE.

THE YOUTH NOTICED THAT THE TATTERED MAN WAS SWINGING UNCERTAINLY ON HIS LEGS, AND THAT HIS FACE HAD TURNED A SHADE OF BLUE.

GOOD LORD! YOU AIN'T GOIN' T' NOT YOU TOO.

NARY DIE. ALL I WANT IS SOME PEA SOUP AND A GOOD BED.

YEH LOOK PRETTY PEEKED YERSELF. I BET YEH'VE GOT A WORSER ONE THAN YEH THINK. YOU BETTER TAKE CARE OF YER HURT. WHERE IS IT LOCATED?

OH, DON'T BOTHER ME!

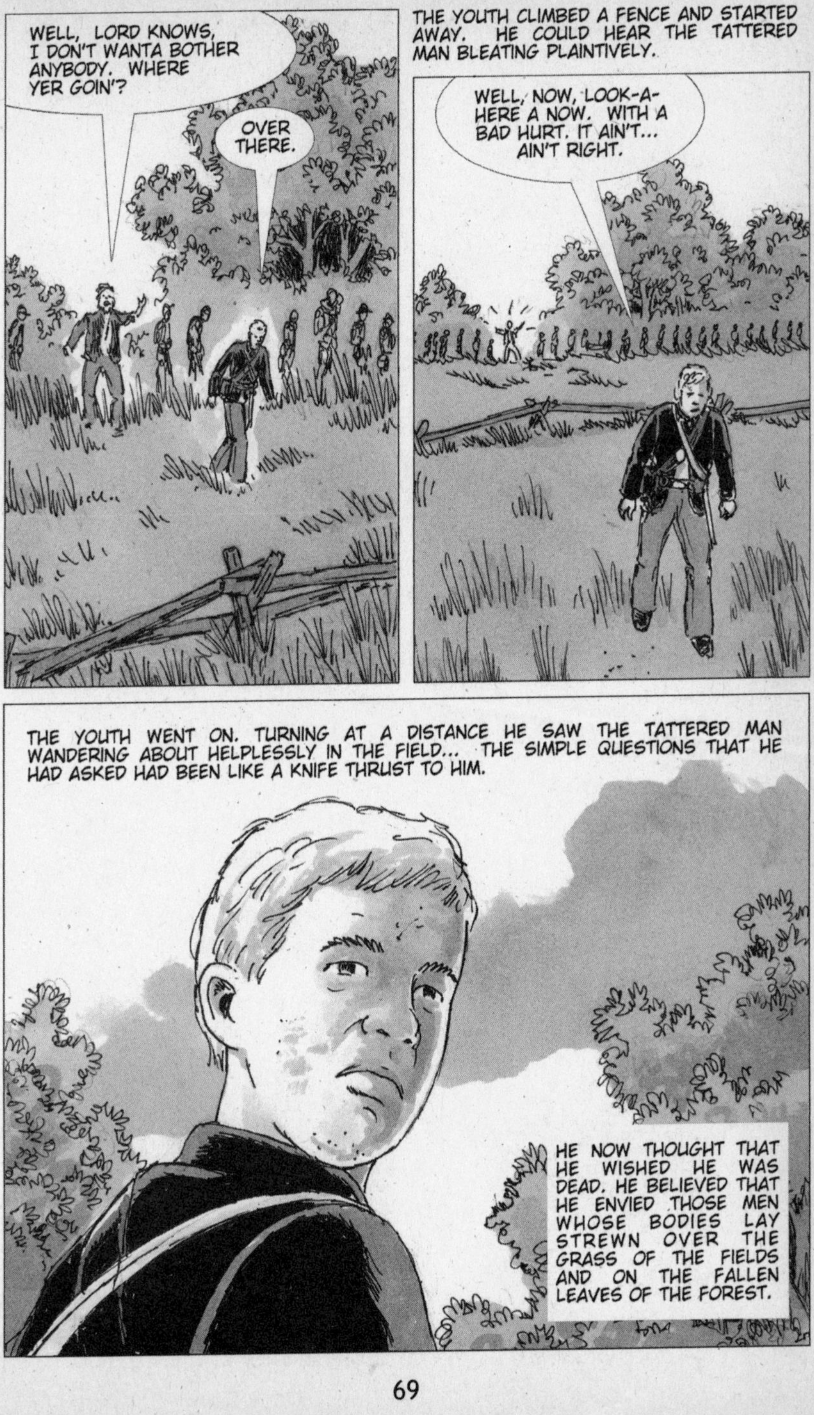
WELL, LORD KNOWS, I DON'T WANTA BOTHER ANYBODY. WHERE YER GOIN'?
OVER THERE.
THE YOUTH CLIMBED A FENCE AND STARTED AWAY. HE COULD HEAR THE TATTERED MAN BLEATING PLAINTIVELY.
WELL, NOW, LOOK-A-HERE A NOW. WITH A BAD HURT. IT AIN'T... AIN'T RIGHT.
THE YOUTH WENT ON. TURNING AT A DISTANCE HE SAW THE TATTERED MAN WANDERING ABOUT HELPLESSLY IN THE FIELD... THE SIMPLE QUESTIONS THAT HE HAD ASKED HAD BEEN LIKE A KNIFE THRUST TO HIM.
HE NOW THOUGHT THAT HE WISHED HE WAS DEAD. HE BELIEVED THAT HE ENVIED THOSE MEN WHOSE BODIES LAY STREWN OVER THE GRASS OF THE FIELDS AND ON THE FALLEN LEAVES OF THE FOREST.

HE BECAME AWARE THAT THE FURNACE ROAR OF THE BATTLE WAS GROWING LOUDER. GREAT BROWN CLOUDS HAD FLOATED TO THE STILL HEIGHTS OF AIR BEFORE HIM. THE ROADWAY WAS NOW A CRYIING MASS OF WAGONS, TEAMS AND MEN...

THE YOUTH FELT COMFORTED IN A MEASURE BY THIS SIGHT. THEY WERE ALL RETREATING.

THEN HE SAW A FORWARD-GOING COLUMN OF INFANTRY ON THE ROAD. IT CAME SWIFTLY ON. THE YOUTH WONDERED WHAT THOSE MEN HAD EATEN THAT THEY COULD BE IN SUCH HASTE TO FORCE THEIR WAY TO GRIM CHANCES OF DEATH.

THE MEN AT THE HEAD BUTTED MULES WITH THEIR MUSKET STOCKS. THEY PRODDED TEAMSTERS INDIFFERENT TO ALL HOWLS.

THE COMMANDS TO MAKE WAY HAD THE RING OF GREAT IMPORTANCE IN THEM.

THE HASTE OF THE COLUMN TO REACH THE BATTLE SEEMED TO THE FORLORN YOUNG MAN TO BE SOMETHING MUCH FINER THAN STOUT FIGHTING. HEROES, HE THOUGHT, COULD FIND EXCUSES IN THE LONG SEETHING LANE.

FOR A FEW MOMENTS HE WANTED TO JOIN THEM IN THEIR FLYING TO THE FRONT. THEN THE DIFFICULTIES OF THE THING BEGAN TO DRAG AT HIM. HE HAD NO RIFLE.

THEY COULD RETIRE WITH PERFECT SELF-RESPECT AND MAKE EXCUSES TO THE STARS.

WELL, RIFLES COULD BE HAD FOR THE PICKING.

IN DESPAIR, HE DECLARED THAT HE WAS NOT LIKE THOSE OTHERS. HE NOW CONCEDED IT TO BE IMPOSSIBLE THAT HE SHOULD EVER BECOME A HERO. HE WAS A CRAVEN LOON. HE DENOUNCED HIMSELF AS A VILLAIN. HE SAID THAT HE WAS THE MOST UNUTTERABLY SELFISH MAN IN EXISTENCE.

HIS MIND PICTURED THE SOLDIERS WHO WOULD PLACE THEIR DEFIANT BODIES BEFORE THE SPEAR OF THE YELLING BATTLE FIEND, AND AS HE SAW THEIR DRIPPING CORPSES ON AN IMAGINED FIELD, HE SAID THAT HE WAS A MURDERER.

SUDDENLY WAVES OF MEN CAME SWEEPING OUT OF THE WOODS AND DOWN THROUGH THE FIELDS. HE KNEW AT ONCE THAT THE STEEL FIBERS HAD BEEN WASHED FROM THEIR HEARTS.

SAY, WHERE DE PLANK ROAD? WHERE DE PLANK ROAD.

THE YOUTH CLUTCHED A MAN B THE THE ARM. HE WAS HEAVING AND PANTING.

WHY, WHY, WHAT'S THE MATTER?

LET GO ME! LET GO ME!

WHY, WHY

WELL, THEN...

THE YOUTH'S FINGERS TURNED TO PASTE UPON THE OTHER'S ARM. HE SAW THE FLAMING WINGS OF LIGHTNINGFLASH BEFORE HIS VISION.

SUDDENLY, HIS LEGS SEEMED TO DIE.

HE FOUGHT AN INTENSE BATTLE WITH HIS BODY. HIS DULL SENSES WISHED HIM TO SWOON AND HE OPPOSED THEM STUBBORNLY.

ONCE HE PUT HIS HAND ON HIS HEAD AND TIMIDLY TOUCHED THE WOUND. THE SCRATCHING PAIN OF THE CONTACT MADE HIM DRAW A LONG BREATH THROUGH HIS CLINCHED TEETH.

HE HURRIED ON IN THE DUSK. THE DAY HAD FADED UNTIL HE COULD BARELY DISTINGUISH A PLACE FOR HIS FEET.

AT LAST HE HEARD A CHEERY VOICE AT HIS SHOULDER.

YEH SEEM T' BE IN A PRETTY BAD WAY, BOY.

UH!

WELL, I'M GOIN' YOUR WAY. TH' HULL GANG IS GOIN' YOUR WAY, AN' I GUESS I KIN GIVE YEH A LIFT.

AS THEY WENT ALONG, THE MAN QUESTIONED THE YOUTH AND ASSISTED HIM WITH THE REPLIES LIKE ONE MANIPULATING THE MIND OF A CHILD. SOMETIMES HE INTERJECTED ANECDOTES.

WHAT REG'MENT DO YEH B'LONG THE? WHAT'S THAT? TH' 304TH NEW YORK?

WHY, WHAT CORPS IS THAT IN? OH, IT IS?

WHY, I THOUGHT THEY WASN'T ENGAGED T'-DAY.

OH, THEY WAS, EH? WELL, PRETTY NEARLY EVERYBODY GOT THEIR SHARE AH FIGHTIN' T'-DAY BY DAD.

THERE WAS SHOOTON' HERE AND SHOOTIN' THERE, IN THE DAMN DARKNESS, UNTIL I COULDN'T TELL T' SAVE M' SOUL WHICH SIDE I WAS ON.

YEH KNOW THERE WAS A BOY KILLED IN MY COMPANY T'-DAY THAT I THOUGHT THE WORLD OF...

WELL, THERE'S WHERE YOUR REG'MENT IS. AN' NOW, GOOD-BY, OL' BOY, GOOD LUCK T' YEH.

74

THE YOUTH WENT SLOWLY TOWARD THE FIRE INDICATED BY HIS DEPARTED FRIEND. AS HE REELED, HE BETHOUGHT HIM OF THE WELCOME HIS COMRADES WOULD GIVE HIM. HE HAD A CONVICTION THAT HE WOULD SOON FEEL IN HIS SORE HEART THE BARBED MISSILES OF RIDICULE. HE HAD NO STRENGTH TO INVENT A TALE; HE WOULD BE A SOFT TARGET.

HALT! HALT!

WHY, HELLO WILSON, YOU... YOU HERE?

THAT YOU, HENRY?

YES, IT'S... IT'S ME.

WELL, WELL. OL' BOY! I'M GLAD TO SEE YEH! I GIVE YEH UP FOR A GONER. I THOUGHT YEH WAS DEAD FOR SURE.

YES, YES. I'VE...I'VE HAD AN AWFUL TIME. I'VE BEEN ALL OVER.... WAY OVER ON TH' RIGHT. TER'BLE FIGHTIN' OVER THERE. I'VE HAD AN AWFUL TIME, I GOT SEPARATED FROM TH' REG'MENT. OVER ON TH' RIGHT, I GOT SHOT. IN TH' HEAD. I NEVER SEEN SUCH FIGHTIN'. AWFUL TIME. I DON'T KNOW HOW I COULD A' GOT SEPARATED FROM THE REG'MENT. I GOT SHOT, TOO.

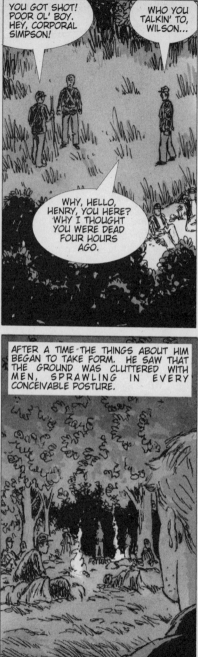

YOU GOT SHOT! POOR OL' BOY. HEY, CORPORAL SIMPSON!

WHO YOU TALKIN' TO, WILSON...

WHY, HELLO, HENRY, YOU HERE? WHY I THOUGHT YOU WERE DEAD FOUR HOURS AGO.

JUST AS I THOUGHT. YEH'VE BEEN GRAZED BY A BALL. IT'S RAISED A QUEER LUMP JEST AS IF SOME FELLER HAD LAMMED YOU WITH A CLUB. NOW, YOU JUST SIT HERE AN' DON'T MOVE, WHILE I GO ROUT OUT THE RELIEF. THEN I'LL SEND WILSON T' TAKE KEER OF YEH.

AFTER A TIME THE THINGS ABOUT HIM BEGAN TO TAKE FORM. HE SAW THAT THE GROUND WAS CLUTTERED WITH MEN, SPRAWLING IN EVERY CONCEIVABLE POSTURE.

THE LOUD SOLDIER FINISHED HIS SENTRY DUTY, AND CLEANED AND BANDAGED THE YOUTH'S WOUND.

THERE. YEH LOOK LIKE THE DEVIL, BUT I BET YEH FEEL BETTER.

THERE, NOW, LIE DOWN AN' GET SOME SLEEP.

THE YOUTH, WITH HIS MANNER OF DOG LIKE OBEDIENCE, STRETCHED OUT WITH A MURMUR OF RELIEF AND COMFORT. THE GROUND FELT LIKE THE SOFTEST COUCH.

HE HAD PERFORMED HIS MISTAKES IN THE DARK, SO HE WAS STILL A MAN.

WHEN THE YOUTH AWOKE IT SEEMED TO HIM THAT HE HAD BEEN ASLEEP FOR A THOUSAND YEARS. GRAY MIST WERE SLOWLY SHIFTING BEFORE THE FIRST EFFORTS OF THE SUN'S RAYS.

WELL, HENRY, OL' MAN. HOW DO YOU FEEL THIS MORNING.

OH, LORD, I FEEL PRETY BAD.

THE YOUTH TOOK NOTE OF A REMARKABLE CHANGE IN HIS COMRADE SINCE THOSE DAYS OF CAMP LIFE UPON THE RIVER BANK.

HE SEEMED NO MORE TO BE CONTINUALLY REGARDING THE PROPORTIONS OF HIS PERSONAL PROWESS. HE WAS NO MORE A LOUD YOUNG SOLDIER.

WELL, HENRY, WHAT D'YEH THINK TH' CHANCES ARE? D'YEH THINK WE'LL WALLOP EM?

DAY B'FORE YESTERDAY, YOU WOULD A' BET YOU'D LICK THE HULL KIT-AN'-BOODLE ALL BY YOURSELF.

WELL, PERHAPS I WOULD.

I THOUGHT WE HANDLED EM PRETTY ROUGH YESTERDAY.

NOT A BIT! WHY, LORD, MAN, YOU DIDN'T SEE NOTHIN' OF THE FIGHT. WHY!...

THEN, A THOUGHT CAME TO HIM.

OH! JIM CONKLIN'S DEAD.

WHAT? IS HE? JIM CONKLIN?

YES. HE'S DEAD. SHOT IN THE SIDE.

YEH DON'T SAY SO. JIM CONKLIN... POOR CUSS!

78

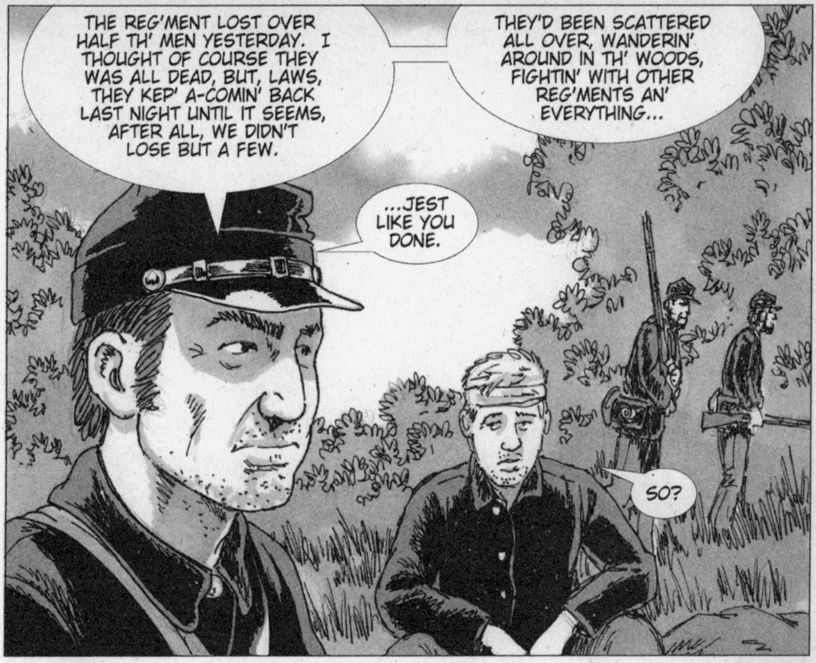
THE REG'MENT LOST OVER HALF TH' MEN YESTERDAY. I THOUGHT OF COURSE THEY WAS ALL DEAD, BUT, LAWS, THEY KEP' A-COMIN' BACK LAST NIGHT UNTIL IT SEEMS, AFTER ALL, WE DIDN'T LOSE BUT A FEW.
THEY'D BEEN SCATTERED ALL OVER, WANDERIN' AROUND IN TH' WOODS, FIGHTIN' WITH OTHER REG'MENTS AN' EVERYTHING...
...JEST LIKE YOU DONE.
SO?

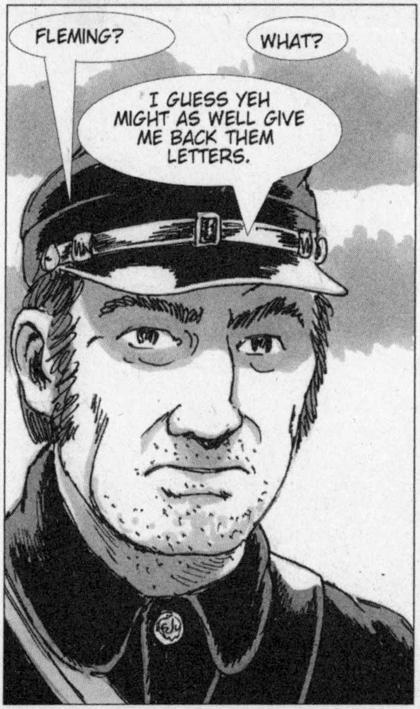
FLEMING?
WHAT?
I GUESS YEH MIGHT AS WELL GIVE ME BACK THEM LETTERS.

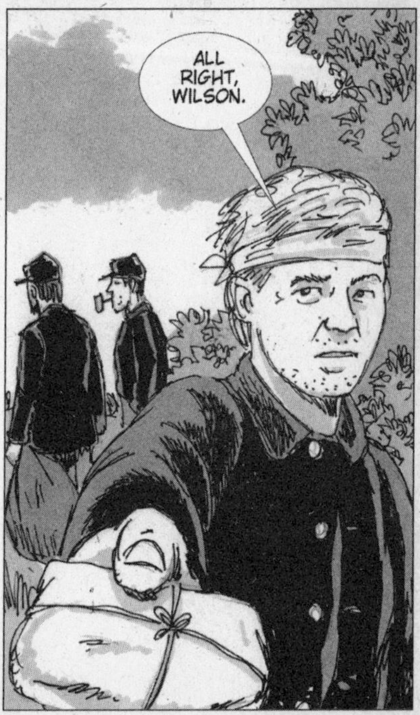
ALL RIGHT, WILSON.

THE YOUTH'S REGIMENT WAS MARCHED TO RELIEVE A COMMAND THAT HAD LAIN LONG IN SOME DAMP TRENCHES. THE MEN TOOK POSITIONS BEHIND A CURVING LINE OF RIFLE PITS THAT HAD BEEN TURNED UP, LIKE A LARGE FURROW, ALONG THE LINE OF THE WOODS.

B'JIMINEY, WE'RE GENERALED BY A LOT A LUNKHEADS!

MORE THAN ONE FELLER HAS SAID THAT T'-DAY.

IF WE FIGHT LIKE THE DEVIL AN' DON'T EVER WHIP, IT MUST BE THE GENERAL'S FAULT.

MEBBE YEH THINK YEH FIT TH' HULL BATTLE YESTIRDAY, FLEMING.

WHY, NO, I DON'T THINK I FOUGHT THE WHOLE BATTLE YESTERDAY.

OH!

THEY WERE MARCHED TO A CLEAR SPACE WHERE REGIMENTS AND BRIGADES, BROKEN AND DETACHED THROUGH THEIR ENCOUNTERS WITH THICKETS, GREW TOGETHER AGAIN AND LINES WERE FACED TOWARD THE PURSUING BARK OF THE ENEMY'S INFANTRY.

WHOOP-A-DADEE!

HERE WE ARE! EVERYBODY FIGHTIN', BLOOD AN' DESTRUCTION!

GOOD GAWD! WE'RE ALWAYS BEING CHASED AROUND LIKE RATS! IT MAKES ME SICK! IT MAKES A MAN FEEL LIKE A KITTEN IN A BAG.

IT'LL ALL WORK OUT IN THE END.

OH, THE DEVIL IT WILL! YOU ALWAYS TALK LIKE DOG-HANGED PARSON...

YOU BOYS SHUT RIGHT UP! THERE'S NO NEED YOU WASTIN' YOUR BREATH IN LONG WINDED ARGUMENTS. ALL YOU GOT TO DO IS FIGHT, AN YOU'LL BE GETTIN' PLENTY IN ABOUT TEN MINUTES.

THERE'S TOO MUCH CHIN MUSIC AN' TOO LITTLE FIGHTIN' IN THIS WAR, ANYHOW.

THE DAY HAD GROWN MORE WHITE, UNTIL THE SUN SHED HIS FULL RADIANCE UPON THE THRONGED FOREST. A SORT OF GUST OF BATTLE CAME SWEEPING TOWARD THAT PART OF THE LINE WHERE LAY THE YOUTH'S REGIMENT.

A SINGLE RIFLE FLASHED IN A THICKET BEFORE THE REGIMENT. IN AN INSTANT IT WAS JOINED BY MANY OTHERS. THERE WAS A MIGHTY SONG OF CLASHES AND CRASHES THAT WENT SWEEPING THROUGH THE WOODS. THE BATTLE SETTLED TO A ROLLING THUNDER.

THERE WAS A PECULIAR KIND OF ATTITUDE IN THE MEN. THEY WERE WORN, EXHAUSTED, HAVING SLEPT BUT LITTLE AND LABORED MUCH, THEY ROLLED THEIR EYES TOWARD THE ADVANCING BATTLE AS THEY STOOD AWAITING THE SHOCK. THEY STOOD AS MEN TIED TO STAKES.

THE ADVANCE OF THE ENEMY HAD SEEMED TO THE YOUTH LIKE A RUTHLESS HUNTING. HE BEGAN TO FUME WITH RAGE AND EXASPERATION. YESTERDAY, WHEN HE HAD IMAGINED THE UNIVERSE TO BE AGAINST HIM, HE HAD HATED IT. TODAY HE HATED THE ARMY OF THE FOE WITH THE SAME GREAT HATRED.

IF THEY KEEP ON CHASING US. BY GAWD, THEY'D BETTER WATCH OUT.

CAN'T STAND TOO MUCH.

IF THEY KEEP ON A-CHASIN' US THEY'LL DRIVE US ALL INTEH TH' RIVER.

THE WIND OF BATTLE HAD SWEPT ALL ABOUT THE REGIMENT, UNTIL ONE RIFLE, INSTANTLY FOLLOWED BY OTHERS, FLASHED IN ITS FRONT.

A MOMENT LATER THE REGIMENT ROARED FORTH IN SUDDEN AND VALIANT RETORT.

THE BLUE SMOKE-SWALLOWED LINE CURLED AND WRITHED LIKE A SNAKE STEPPED UPON. IT SWUNG IT'S ENDS TO AND FRO IN THE AGONY OF FEAR AND RAGE.

THE FLAMES FIT HIM, AND THE HOT SMOKE BROILED HIS SKIN.

HIS RIFLE BARREL GREW SO HOT THAT ORDINARILY HE COULD NOT HAVE BORNE IT UPON HIS PALMS

BUT HE KEPT ON STUFFING CARTRIDGES INTO IT, AND POUNDING THEM WITH HIS CLANKING, BENDING RAMROD.

IF HE AIMED AT SOME CHARGING FORM THROUGH THE SMOKE, HE PULLED THE TRIGGER WITH A FIERCE GRUNT...

...AS IF HE WAS DEALING A BLOW OF THE FIST WITH ALL HIS STRENGTH.

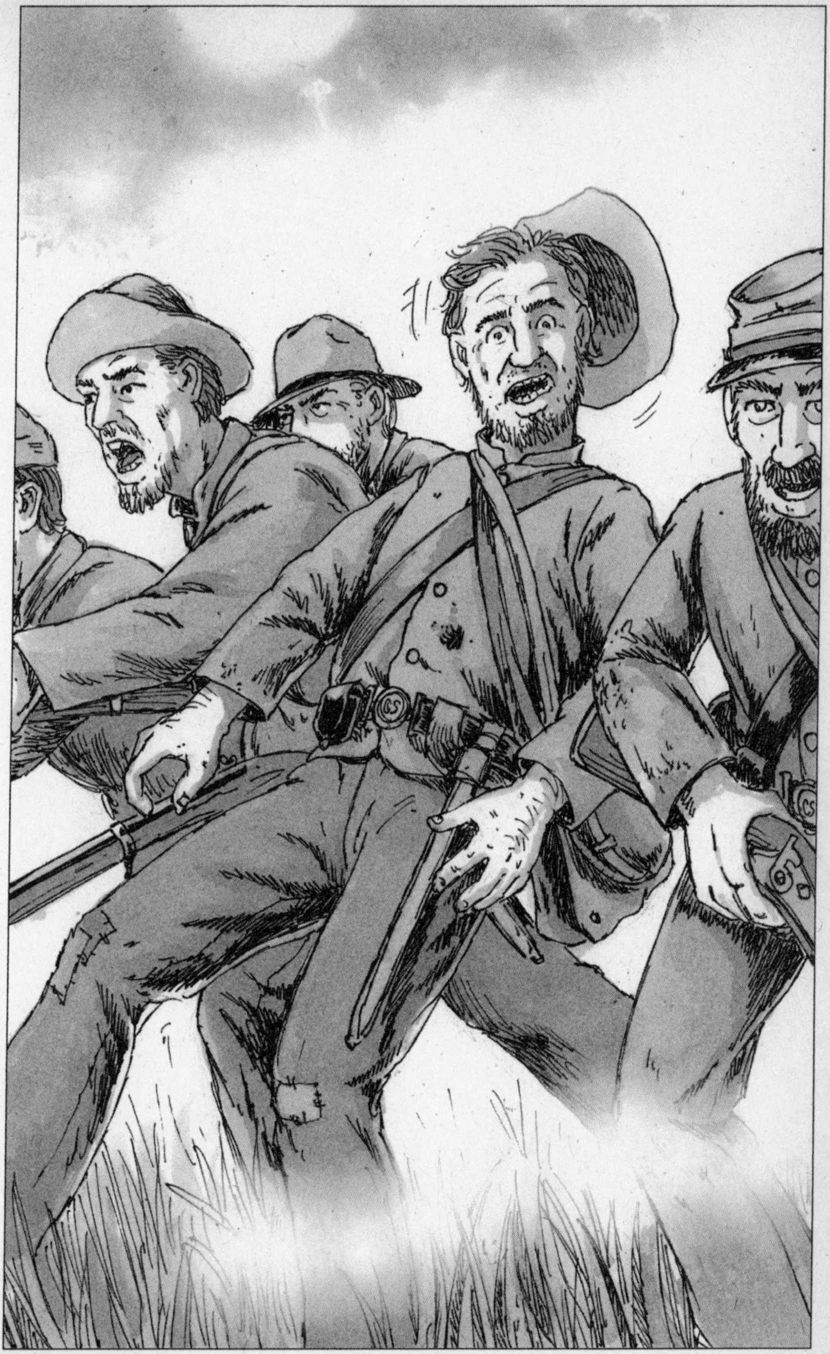

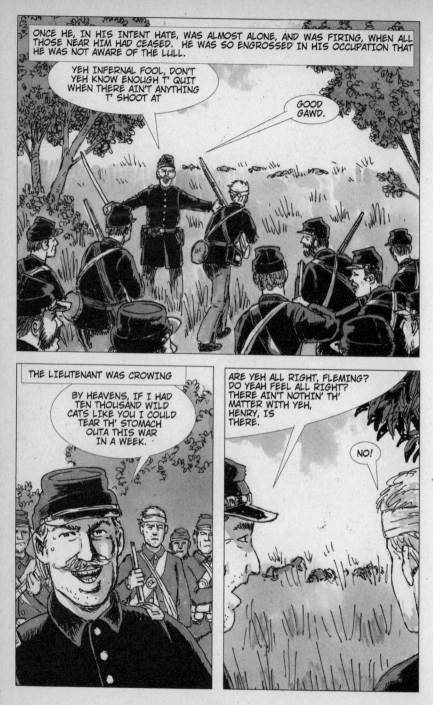

ONCE HE, IN HIS INTENT HATE, WAS ALMOST ALONE, AND WAS FIRING, WHEN ALL THOSE NEAR HIM HAD CEASED. HE WAS SO ENGROSSED IN HIS OCCUPATION THAT HE WAS NOT AWARE OF THE LULL.

YEH INFERNAL FOOL, DON'T YEH KNOW ENOUGH T' QUIT WHEN THERE AIN'T ANYTHING T' SHOOT AT

GOOD GAWD.

THE LIEUTENANT WAS CROWING

BY HEAVENS, IF I HAD TEN THOUSAND WILD CATS LIKE YOU I COULD TEAR TH' STOMACH OUTA THIS WAR IN A WEEK.

ARE YEH ALL RIGHT, FLEMING? DO YEAH FEEL ALL RIGHT? THERE AIN'T NOTHIN' TH' MATTER WITH YEH, HENRY, IS THERE.

NO!

THERE WAS SOME GRIM REJOICING BY THE MEN.

I BET THIS ARMY'LL NEVER SEE ANOTHER NEW REG'MENT LIKE US!

YOU BET A DOG, A WOMAN, AN A WALNUT TREE, TH' MORE YEH BEAT EM, TH' BETTER THEY BE. THA'S LIKE US.

LOST A PILAR MEN, THEY DID. IF AN' OL' WOMAN SWEP' UP TH' WOODS SHE'D GET A DUSTPANFULL.'

YES, AN' IF SHE'LL COME AROUND AG'IN ABOUT AN HOUR SHE'LL GET A PILE MORE.

THE FOREST STILL BORE ITS BURDEN OF CLAMOR. FROM OFF UROM OFF UNDER THE TREES CAME THE ROLLING CLATTER OF MUSKETRY.

89

THERE WAS ONE SHOT THROUGH THE BODY, WHO RAISED A CRY OF BITTER AND PAINFUL LAMENTATIONS WHEN CAME THIS LULL. PERHAPS HE HAD BEEN CALLING OUT DURING THE FIGHTING ALSO, BUT AT THAT TIME NO ONE HAD HEARD HIM. BUT NOW THE MEN TURNED AT THE WOEFUL COMPLAINTS OF HIM UPON THE GROUND.

WHO IS IT? WHO IS IT?

IT'S JIMMIE ROGERS. JIMMIE ROGERS!

THE CHESTS OF THE MEN STRAINED FOR A BIT OF FRESHNESS, AND THEIR THROATS CRAVED WATER.

THE YOUTH'S FRIEND HAD A GEOGRAPHICAL ILLUSION CONCERNING A STREAM, AND HE OBTAINED PERMISSION TO GO FOR SOME WATER. IMMEDIATELY CANTEENS WERE SHOWERED UPON HIM.

FILL MINE, WILL YEH?

BRING ME SOME TOO.

AND ME TOO.

THE YOUTH WENT WITH HIS FRIEND, FEELING A DESIRE TO THROW HIS HEATED BODY ONTO THE STREAM AND, SOAKING THERE, DRINK QUARTS.

NO WATER HERE.

THEY MADE A HURRIED SEARCH FOR THE SUPPOSED STREAM, BUT DID NOT FIND IT.

THEY TURNED WITHOUT DELAY AND BEGAN TO RETRACE THEIR STEPS. FROM THEIR POSITION AS THEY AGAIN FACED TOWARD THE PLACE OF FIGHTING, THEY COULD OF COURSE COMPREHEND A GREATER AMOUNT OF THE BATTLE THAN THEIR VISIONS HAD BLURRED BY THE HURLING SMOKE OF THE LINE.

THEY COULD SEE DARK STRETCHES WINDING ALONG THE LAND, AND ON ONE CLEARED SPACE THERE WAS A ROW OF GUNS MAKING GRAY CLOUDS, WHICH WERE FILLED WITH LARGE FLASHES OF ORANGE-COLORED FLAMES.

91

THE YOUTH AND HIS COMPANION SAW WHO THEY KNEW AS THEIR GENERAL OF DIVISION AND HIS STAFF. ANOTHER OFFICER, RIDING WITH THE SKILLFUL ABANDON OF A COWBOY, GALLOPED HIS HORSE TO A POSITION DIRECTLY BEFORE THE GENERAL.

TH' ENEMY'S FORMIN' OVER THERE FOR ANOTHER CHARGE...

IT'LL BE DIRECTED TOWARD WHITERSIDE, AN' I FEAR THEY'LL BREAK THROUGH THERE UNLESS WE WORK LIKE HELL T' STOP THEM.

WELL, I HAD TO ORDER TH' 12TH TO HELP THE 76TH...

ALL I'VE GOT LEFT IN THE 304TH, AND THEY FIGHT LIKE A LOT OF MULE-DRIVERS...

GET THEM READY, THEN. I'LL WATCH DEVELOPMENTS FROM HERE, AN' SEND THE WORD WHEN T' START THEM. IT'LL HAPPEN IN FIVE MINUTES.

I DON'T BELIEVE MANY OF YOUR MULE-DRIVERS WILL GET BACK.

92

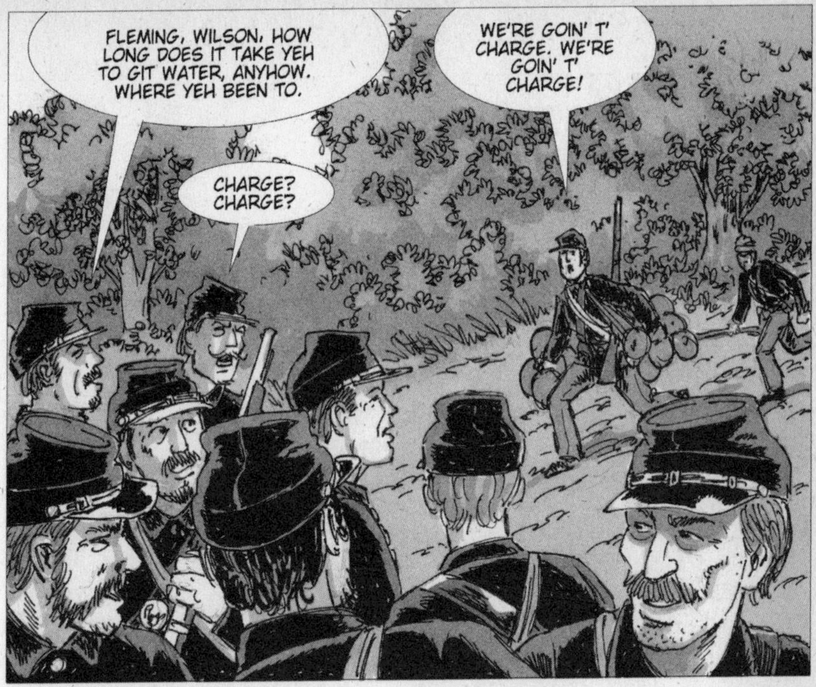
FLEMING, WILSON, HOW LONG DOES IT TAKE YEH TO GIT WATER, ANYHOW. WHERE YEH BEEN TO.
CHARGE? CHARGE?
WE'RE GOIN' T' CHARGE. WE'RE GOIN' T' CHARGE!

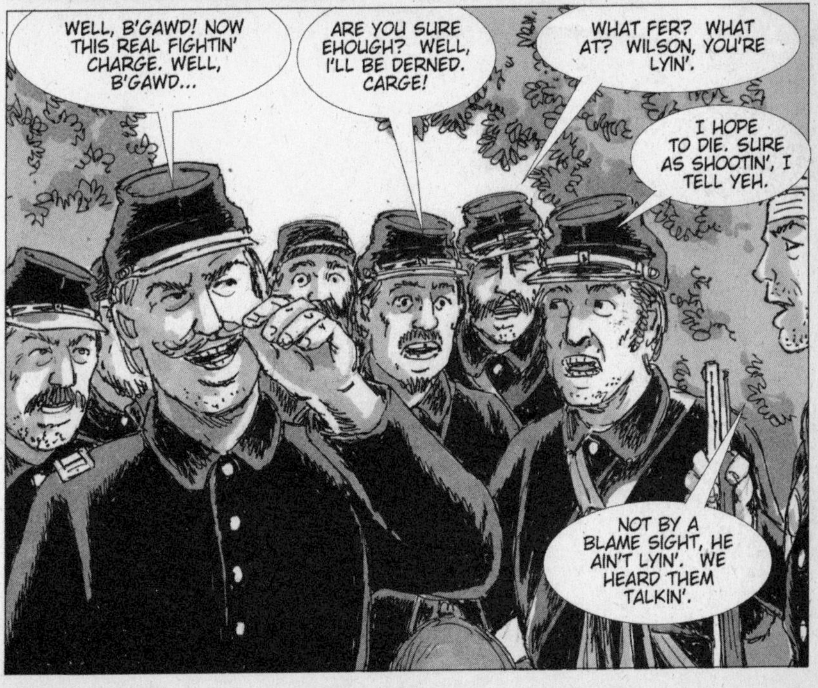
WELL, B'GAWD! NOW THIS REAL FIGHTIN' CHARGE. WELL, B'GAWD...
ARE YOU SURE EHOUGH? WELL, I'LL BE DERNED. CARGE!
WHAT FER? WHAT AT? WILSON, YOU'RE LYIN'.
I HOPE TO DIE. SURE AS SHOOTIN', I TELL YEH.
NOT BY A BLAME SIGHT, HE AIN'T LYIN'. WE HEARD THEM TALKIN'.

THE YOUTH, TURNING, SHOT A QUICK, INQUIRING GLANCE AT HIS FRIEND. THE LATTER RETURNED TO HIM THE SAME MANNER OF LOOK. THEY WERE THE ONLY ONES WHO POSSESSED AN INTER KNOWLEDGE.

MULE-DRIVERS.

HELL T' PAY.

DON'T BELIEVE MANY WILL GET BACK.

IT WAS AN IRONIC SECRET. STILL, THEY SAW NO HESITATION IN EACH OTHERS FACES, AND THEN NODDED A MUTE AND UNPROTESTING ASSENT.

THE YOUTH STARED AT THE LAND IN FRONT OF HIM. ITS FOLIAGES NOW SEEMED TO VEIL POWERS AND HORRORS.

HE WAS UNAWARE OF THE MACHINERY OF ORDERS THAT STARTED THE CHARGE, ALTHOUGH FROM THE CORNERS OF HIS EYES HE SAW AN OFFICER COME GALLOPING, WAVING HIS HAT.

95

THE LINE FELL SLOWLY FORWARD LIKE A TOPPLING WALL, AND, WITH A CONVULSIVE GASP THAT WAS INTENDED FOR A CHEER, THE REGIMENT BEGAN ITS JOURNEY.

AS THE REGIMENT SWUNG FROM ITS POSITION OUT INTO A CLEARED SPACE THE WOODS AND THICKETS BEFORE IT AWAKENED. YELLOW FLAMES LEAPED FROM MANY DIRECTIONS. THE FOREST MADE A TREMENDOUS OBJECTION.

THE LINE LURCHED STRAIGHT FOR A MOMENT. THEN THE RIGHT WING SWUNG FORWARD; IT IN TURN WAS SURPASSED BY THE LEFT. AFTERWARD THE CENTER CAREERED TO THE FRONT UNTIL THE REGIMENT WAS A WEDGE-SHAPED MASS, BUT AN INSTANT LATER THE OPPOSITION OF THE BUSHES, TREES, AND UNEVEN PLACES ON THE GROUND SPLIT THE COMMAND AND SCATTERED IT INTO DETACHED CLUSTERS.

THE SONG OF THE BULLETS WAS IN THE AIR AND SHELLS SNARLED AMONG THE TREETOPS.

MEN PUNCHED BY BULLETS FELL IN GROTESQUE AGONIES. THE REGIMENT LEFT A COHERENT TRAIL OF BODIES.

ONE SHELL TUMBLED DIRECTLY INTO THE MIDDLE OF A HURRYING GROUP AND EXPLODED IN CRIMSON FURY.

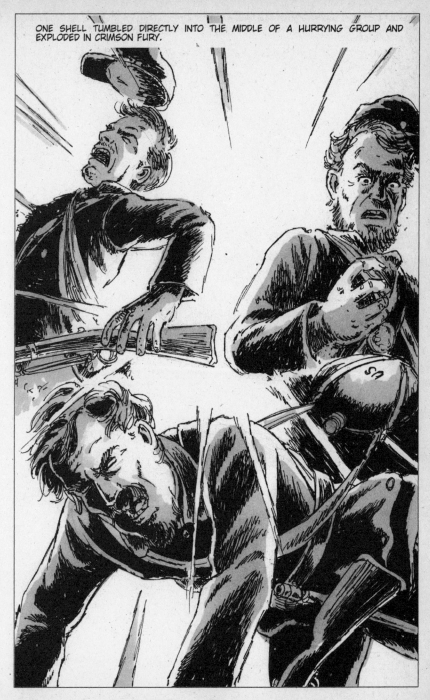

THE OPPOSING INFANTRY'S LINES WERE DEFINED BY THE GRAY WALLS AND FRINGES OF SMOKE.

THERE WAS A FRENZY MADE FROM THIS FURIOUS RUSH. THE MEN, PITCHING FORWARD INSANELY, HAD BURST INTO CHEERING, MOBLIKE AND BARBARIC, BUT TUNED IN STRANGE KEYS THAT CAN AROUSE THE DULLARD AND THE STOIC.

IT MADE A MAD ENTHUSIASM THAT, IT SEEMED, WOULD BE INCAPABLE OF CHECKING ITSELF BEFORE GRANITE AND BRASS.

PRESENTLY THE STRAINING PACE ATE UP THE ENERGIES OF THE MEN . AS IF BY AGREEMENT, THE LEADERS BEGAN TO SLACKEN SPEED.

SINCE MUCH OF THEIR STRENGTH AND THEIR BREATH HAD VANISHED, THEY RETURNED TO CAUTION. THEY WERE BECOMING MEN AGAIN.

THE YOUTH HAD A VAGUE BELIEF THAT HE HAD RUN MILES, AND HE THOUGHT IN A WAY, THAT HE WAS NOW IN SOME NEW AND UNKNOWN LAND.

101

THE MEN, HALTED, HAD OPPORTUNITY TO SEE SOME OF THEIR COMRADES DROPPING WITH MOANS AND SHRIEKS. A FEW LAY UNDER FOOT, STILL OR WAILING. AND NOW FOR AN INSTANT THE MEN STOOD, THEIR RIFLES SLACK IN THEIR HANDS, AND WATCHED THE REGIMENT DWINDLE.

THEY APPEARED DAZED AND STUPID.

THEN, ABOVE THE SOUND OF THE OUTSIDE COMMOTION, AROSE THE ROAR OF THE LIEUTENANT. HE STRODE SUDDENLY FORTH, HIS INFANTILE FEATURES BLACK WITH RAGE.

COME ON, YEH FOOLS!

COME ON! YOU CAN'T STAY HERE!

YOU MUST COME ON!

KRAK!

KA-POW!

POW!

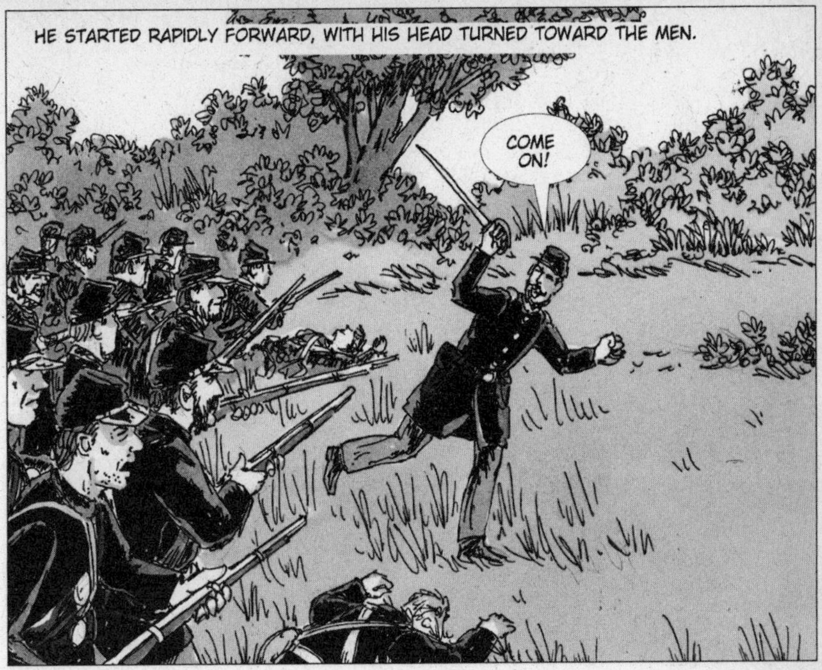
HE STARTED RAPIDLY FORWARD, WITH HIS HEAD TURNED TOWARD THE MEN.
COME ON!

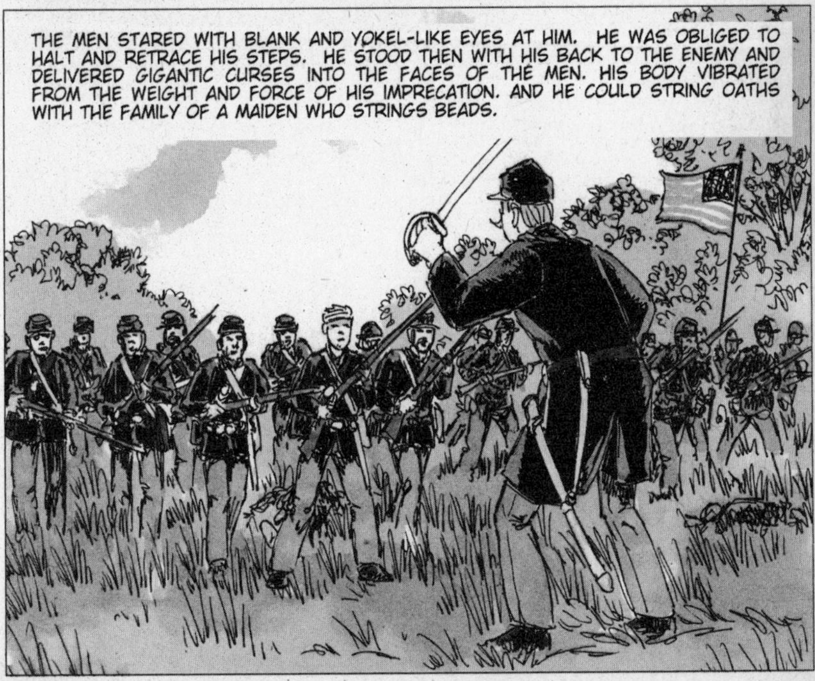
THE MEN STARED WITH BLANK AND YOKEL-LIKE EYES AT HIM. HE WAS OBLIGED TO HALT AND RETRACE HIS STEPS. HE STOOD THEN WITH HIS BACK TO THE ENEMY AND DELIVERED GIGANTIC CURSES INTO THE FACES OF THE MEN. HIS BODY VIBRATED FROM THE WEIGHT AND FORCE OF HIS IMPRECATION. AND HE COULD STRING OATHS WITH THE FAMILY OF A MAIDEN WHO STRINGS BEADS.

THE FRIEND OF THE YOUTH AROUSED. LURCHING SUDDENLY FORWARD AND DROPPING TO HIS KNEES, HE FIRED AN ANGRY SHOT AT THE PERSISTENT WOODS.

THIS ACTION AWAKENED THE MEN. THEY HUDDLED NO MORE LIKE SHEEP. THEY SEEMED SUDDENLY TO BETHINK THEM OF THEIR WEAPONS, AND AT ONCE COMMENCED FIRING.

BELABORED BY THEIR OFFICERS, THEY BEGAN TO MOVE FORWARD. THE REGIMENT, LIKE A CART INVOLVED IN MUD AND MUDDLE, STARTED UNEVENLY WITH MANY JOLTS AND JERKS. THE MEN STOPPED NOW EVERY FEW PACES TO FIRE AND LOAD, AND IN THIS MANNER MOVED SLOWLY ON FROM TREES TO TREES.

THE FLAMING OPPOSITION IN THEIR FRONT GREW WITH THEIR ADVANCE UNTIL IT SEEMED THAT ALL FORWARD WAYS WERE BARRED BY THE THIN LEAPING TONGUES, AND OFF TO THE RIGHT AN OMINOUS DEMONSTRATION COULD SOMETIMES BE DIMLY DISCERNED.

THE SMOKE LATELY GENERATED WAS IN CONFUSING CLOUDS THAT MADE IT DIFFICULT FOR THE REGIMENT TO PROCEED WITH INTELLIGENCE.

AS HE PASSED THROUGH EACH CURLING MASS THE YOUTH WONDERED WHAT WOULD CONFRONT HIM ON THE FARTHER SIDE.

THE COMMAND WENT PAINFULLY FORWARD UNTIL AN OPEN SPACE INTERPOSED BETWEEN THEM AND THE LURID LINES. HERE, CROUCHED AND COWERING BEHIND SOME TREES, THE MEN CLUNG WITH DESPERATION, AS IF THREATENED BY A WAVE.

THEY LOOKED WILD EYED, AND AS IF AMAZED AT THIS FURIOUS DISTURBANCE THEY HAD STIRRED. IN THE STORM THERE WAS AN IRONICAL EXPRESSION OF THEIR IMPORTANCE. THE FACES OF THE MEN, TOO, SHOWED A LACK OF A CERTAIN FEELING OF RESPONSIBILITY FOR BEING THERE.

AS THEY HALTED THUS THE LIEUTENANT AGAIN BEGAN TO BELLOW PROFANELY. REGARDLESS OF THE VINDICTIVE THREATS OF THE BULLETS, HE WENT ABOUT COAXING, BERATING, AND BEDAMNING.

HE SWORE BY ALL POSSIBLE DEITIES.

HE GRABBED THE YOUTH BY THE ARM.

COME ON, YEH LUNKHEAD!

WE'LL ALL GET KILLED IF WE STAY HERE

WE'VE ONLY GOT T' GO ACROSS THAT LOT.

CROSS THERE?

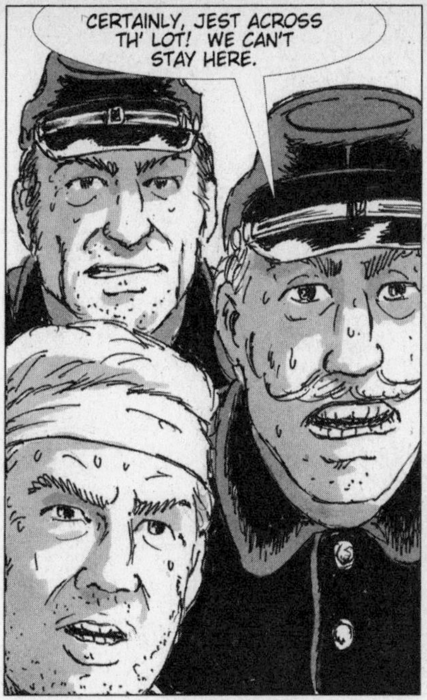
CERTAINLY, JEST ACROSS TH' LOT! WE CAN'T STAY HERE.

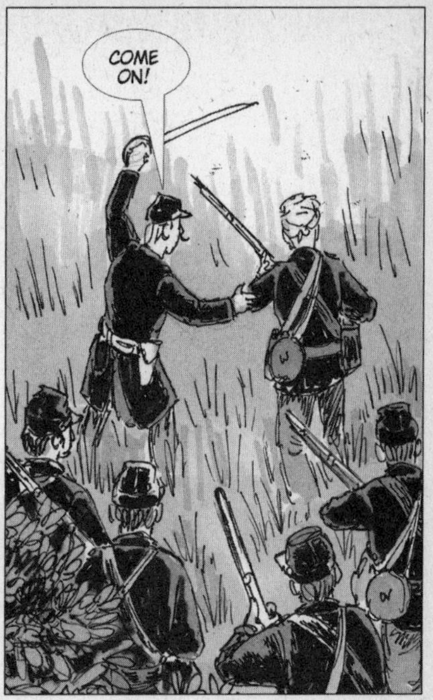
COME ON!

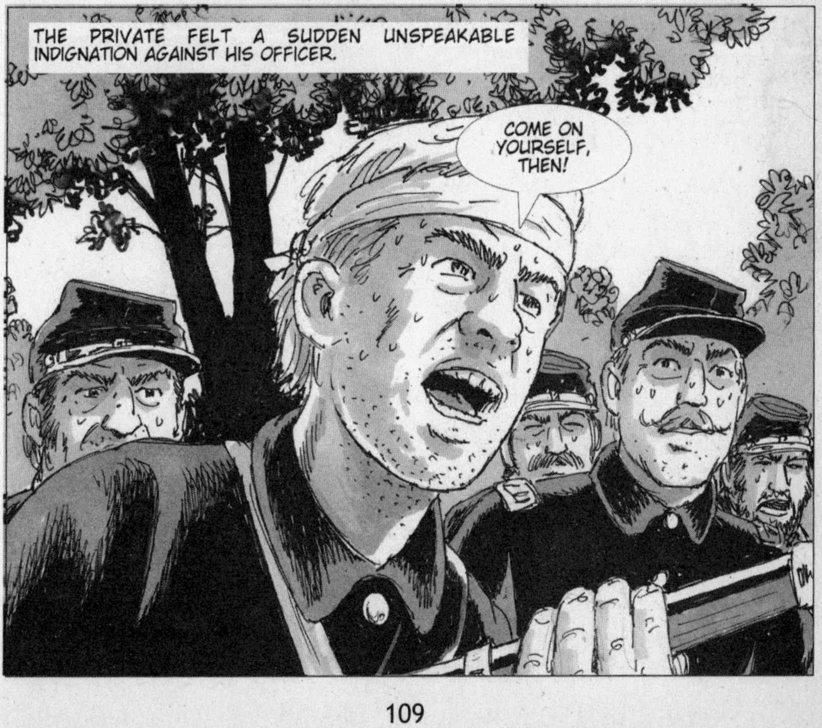
THE PRIVATE FELT A SUDDEN UNSPEAKABLE INDIGNATION AGAINST HIS OFFICER.
COME ON YOURSELF, THEN!

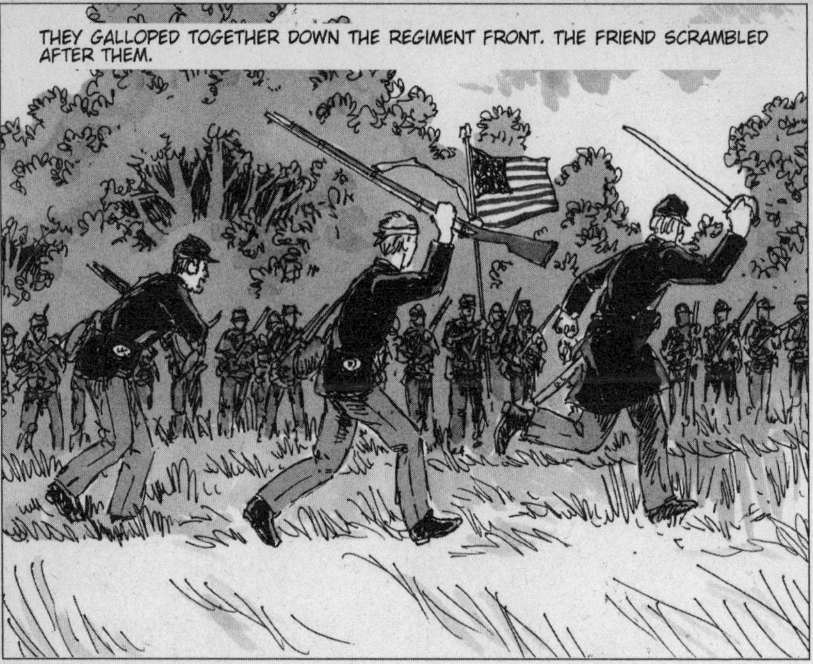
THEY GALLOPED TOGETHER DOWN THE REGIMENT FRONT. THE FRIEND SCRAMBLED AFTER THEM.

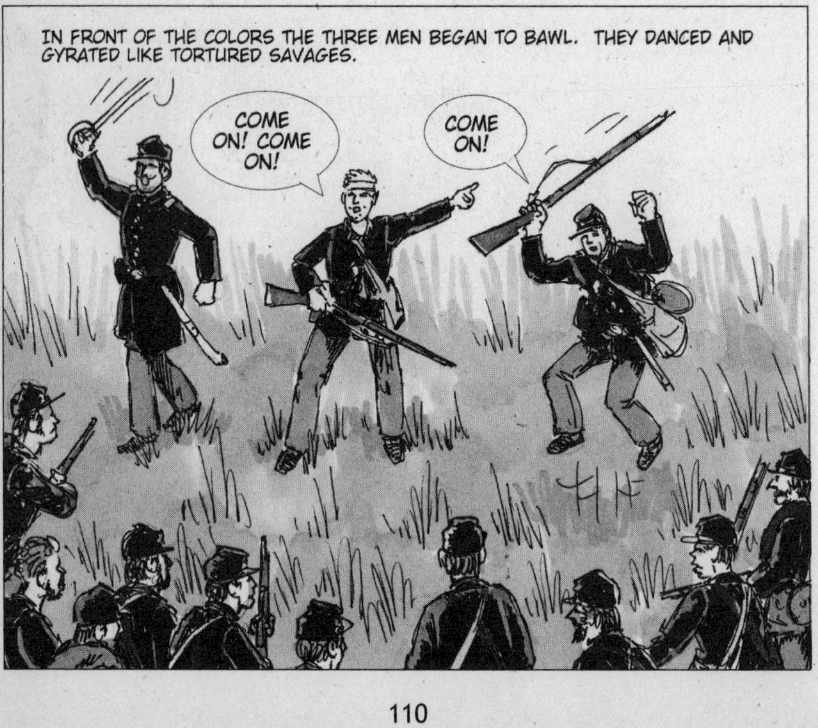
IN FRONT OF THE COLORS THE THREE MEN BEGAN TO BAWL. THEY DANCED AND GYRATED LIKE TORTURED SAVAGES.
COME ON! COME ON!
COME ON!

THE FLAG, OBEDIENT TO THESE APPEALS, BENDED ITS GLITTERING
FORM AND SWEPT TOWARD THEM.

THE MEN WAVERED IN INDECISION FOR A MOMENT, AND THEN WITH A LONG,
WAILFUL CRY THE DILAPIDATED REGIMENT SURGED FORWARD AND BEGAN ITS
NEW JOURNEY.

OVER THE FIELD WENT THE SCURRYING MASS. IT WAS A HANDFUL OF MEN SPLATTERED
INTO THE FACES OF THE ENEMY. TOWARD IT INSTANTLY SPRANG THE YELLOW TONGUES. A
VAST QUANTITY OF BLUE SMOKE HUNG BEFORE THEM. A MIGHTY BANGING MADE EARS
VALUELESS.

THE YOUTH RAN LIKE A MAD MAN TO REACH THE WOODS BEFORE A BULLET COULD DISCOVER HIM, HE DUCKED HIS HEAD LOW, LIKE A FOOTBALL PLAYER.

WITHIN HIM, AS HE HURLED HIMSELF FORWARD, WAS BORN A LOVE, A DESPAIRING FONDNESS FOR THIS FLAG WHICH WAS NEAR HIM.

IT WAS A CREATION OF BEAUTY AND INVULNERABILITY. IT WAS A GODDESS, RADIANT, THAT BENDED ITS FORM WITH AN IMPERIOUS GESTURE TO HIM. IT WAS A WOMAN, RED AND WHITE, HATING AND LIVING, THAT CALLED HIM WITH THE VOICE OF HIS HOPES.

BECAUSE NO HARM COULD COME TO IT, HE ENDOWED IT WITH POWER. HE KEPT NEAR, AS IF IT COULD BE A SAVER OF LIVES, AND AN IMPLORING CRY WENT UP FROM HIS MIND.

IN THE MAD SCRAMBLE HE WAS AWARE THAT THE COLOR SERGEANT FLINCHED SUDDENLY, AS IF STRUCK BY A BLUDGEON. HE FALTERED, AND THEN BECAME MOTIONLESS, SAVE FOR HIS QUIVERING KNEES.

KRACK!

POW!

KRACK!

POW!

POK!

HE MADE A SPRING AND A CLUTCH AT THE POLE. AT THE SAME INSTANT HIS FRIEND GRABBED IT FROM THE OTHER SIDE.

THEY JERKED AT IT, STOUT AND FURIOUS, BUT THE COLOR SERGEANT WAS DEAD, AND THE CORPSE WOULD NOT RELINQUISH ITS TRUST.

FOR A MOMENT THERE WAS A GRIM ENCOUNTER.

THE DEAD MAN, SWINGING WITH BENDED BACK, SEEMED TO BE OBSTINATELY TUGGED, IN LUDICROUS AND AWFUL WAYS, FOR THE POSSESSION OF THE FLAG.

IT WAS PAST IN AN INSTANT OF TIME. THEY WRENCHED THE FLAG FURIOUSLY FROM THE DEAD MAN.

THE CORPSE SWAYED FORWARD WITH BOWED HEAD. ONE ARM SWUNG HIGH, AND THE CURVED HAND FELL WITH HEAVY PROTEST ON THE FRIEND'S UNHEEDING SHOULDER.

THE YOUTH AND HIS FRIEND HAD A SMALL SCUFFLE OVER THE FLAG.

GIVE IT T' ME!

NO! LET ME KEEP IT!

EACH FELT SATISFIED WITH THE OTHER'S POSSESSION OF IT, BUT HAD TO SHOW HIS WILLINGNESS TO FURTHER RISK.

THE YOUTH ROUGHLY PUSHED HIS FRIEND AWAY.

THE REGIMENT RESUMED ITS MARCH AGAIN, CURVING AMONG THE TREE TRUNKS. THE GREATER PART OF THE MEN, DISCOURAGED, THEIR SPIRITS WORN BY THE TURMOIL, ACTED AS IF STUNNED.

SHOOT INTO EM! SHOOT INTO EM, DAMN THEIR SOULS!

THE LIEUTENANT HAD BEEN SHOT IN THE ARM. IT HUNG STRAIGHT AND RIGID. OCCASIONALLY HE WOULD CEASE TO REMEMBER IT, AND BE ABOUT TO EMPHASIZE AN OATH WITH A SWEEPING GESTURE. THE MULTIPLIED PAIN CAUSED HIM TO SWEAR WITH INCREDIBLE POWER.

116

THE REGIMENT HAD RUN DOWN. THE MEN, HAVING HURLED THEMSELVES IN PROJECTILE FASHION, HAD PRESENTLY EXTENDED THEIR FORCES. THEY SLOWLY RETREATED, WITH THEIR FACES STILL TOWARD THE SPLUTTERING WOODS, AND THEIR HOT RIFLES STILL REPLYING TO THE DIN.

THE YOUTH HARANGUED HIS FELLOWS, PUSHING AGAINST THEIR CHEST WITH HIS FREE HAND. TO THOSE HE KNEW WELL HE MADE FRANTIC APPEALS, BESEECHING THEM BY NAME. HE WANTED REVENGE UPON THE OFFICER WHO HAD REFERRED TO HIM AND HIS FELLOWS AS MULE DRIVERS.

AND NOW THE RETREAT OF THE MULE DRIVERS WAS A MARCH OF SHAME TO HIM.

BUT THE REGIMENT WAS A MACHINE RUNDOWN. IT WAS DIFFICULT TO THINK OF REPUTATION WHEN OTHERS WERE THINKING OF SKINS. WOUNDED MEN WERE LEFT CRYING WHERE THEY LAY.

THE WAY SEEMED ETERNAL. IN THE CLOUDED HAZE MEN BECAME PANIC STRICKEN WITH THE THOUGHT THAT THEY MIGHT HAVE LOST THEIR PATH AND WERE PROCEEDING IN A PERILOUS DIRECTION.

THEY SUDDENLY REALIZED THAT THEY HAD BEEN FIRED UPON FROM POINTS WHICH THEY HAD CONSIDERED TO BE TOWARD THEIR OWN LINES.

118

THE OFFICERS LABORED LIKE POLITICIANS TO BEAT THE MASS INTO A PROPER CIRCLE TO FACE THE MENACES. THE MEN CURLED INTO DEPRESSIONS AND FITTED THEMSELVES SNUGLY BEHIND WHATEVER WOULD FRUSTRATE A BULLET.

THE YOUTH NOTED WITH VAGUE SURPRISE THE LIEUTENANT WAS STANDING MUTELY. HE WONDERED WHAT HAD HAPPENED TO HIS VOCAL ORGANS THAT HE HAD NO MORE CURSES.

THERE WAS SOMETHING CURIOUS IN THIS LITTLE INTENT PAUSE. HE WAS LIKE A BABE WHICH, HAVING WEPT ITS FILL, RAISES ITS EYES AND FIXES THEM UPON A DISTANT TOY.

THEN HIS EYES WIDENED, AND HIS SOFT UNDER LIP QUIVERED FROM SELF-WHISPERED WORDS.

119

THE HAZE OF TREACHERY DISCLOSED A BODY OF ENEMY SOLDIERS. THEY WERE SO NEAR THAT THE YOUTH COULD SEE THEIR FEATURES. THEIR UNIFORMS WERE RATHER GAY IN EFFECT, BEING LIGHT GRAY, ACCENTED WITH A BRILLIANT-HUES FACING. TOO, THE CLOTHING SEEMED NEW.

HERE THEY COME!

RIGHT ONTO US, B'GAWD!

THE TWO BODIES OF TROOPS EXCHANGED BLOWS IN THE MANNER OF A PAIR OF BOXERS. THE FAST ANGRY FIRING WENT BACK AND FORTH....

THE MEN IN BLUE WERE INTENT WITH THE DESPAIR OF THEIR CIRCUMSTANCES AND THEY SEIZED UPON THE REVENGE TO BE HAD AT CLOSE RANGE. THE YOUTH HAD A SWEET THOUGHT THAT IF THE ENEMY WAS ABOUT TO SWALLOW THE REGIMENT, AT LEAST THEY HAD THE CONSOLATION OF GOING DOWN WITH BRISTLES FORWARD.

THE BLOWS OF THE ANTAGONIST BEGAN TO GROW MORE WEAK. WHEN THE MIST LIFTED, THEY SAW A GROUND VACANT OF FIGHTERS EXCEPT FOR THE CORPSES THAT LAY THROWN AND TWISTED INTO FANTASTIC SHAPES UPON THE SWARD.

THE MEN IN BLUE SPRANG OUT FROM BEHIND THEIR COVER, SOME OF THEM DANCING WITH JOY. THIS SMALL DUEL SHOWED THEM THAT THE PROPORTIONS WERE NOT IMPOSSIBLE. THE IMPETOUS OF ENTHUSIASM WAS THEIRS AGAIN. THEY GAZED ABOUT THEM WITH LOOKS OF UPLIFTED PRIDE, FEELING NEW TRUST IN THE GRIM, ALWAYS CONFIDENT WEAPONS IN THEIR HANDS.

AND THEY WERE MEN.

ALL WAYS SEEMED OPEN TO THEM. IN THE DISTANCE THERE WERE MANY COLOSSAL NOISES, BUT IN ALL THIS PART OF THE FIELD THERE WAS A SUDDEN STILLNESS....

IN THIS LAST LENGTH OF JOURNEY THE MEN BEGAN TO SHOW STRANGE EMOTIONS. THEY HURRIED WITH NERVOUS FEAR AND BACKWARD LOOKS OF PERTURBATION.

IT WAS PERHAPS THAT THEY DREADED TO BE KILLED IN INSIGNIFICANT WAYS AFTER THE TIMES FOR PROPER MILITARY DEATHS HAD PASSED.

AS THEY APPROACHED THEIR OWN LINES THERE WAS SOME SARCASM EXHIBITED ON THE PART OF A GAUNT AND BRONZED REGIMENT THAT LAY RESTING IN THE SHADE OF THE TREES.

WHERE TH' HELL YEH BEEN?

WHAT YEH COMIN' BACK FER?

WAS IT WARM OUT THEIR, BOYS?

THE YOUTH'S TENDER FLESH WAS DEEPLY STUNG BY THESE REMARKS.

THEY TURNED WHEN THEY ARRIVED AT THEIR POSITION TO REGARD THE GROUND OVER WHICH THEY HAD JUST CHARGED. THE YOUTH WAS SMITTEN WITH ASTONISHMENT.

THE DISTANCE NOW SEEMED TRIVIAL AND RIDICULOUS.

124

THE OFFICER WHO HAD FIRST REFERRED TO THEM AS MULE DRIVERS CAME GALLOPING UP TO THEIR REGIMENT'S COMMANDER...

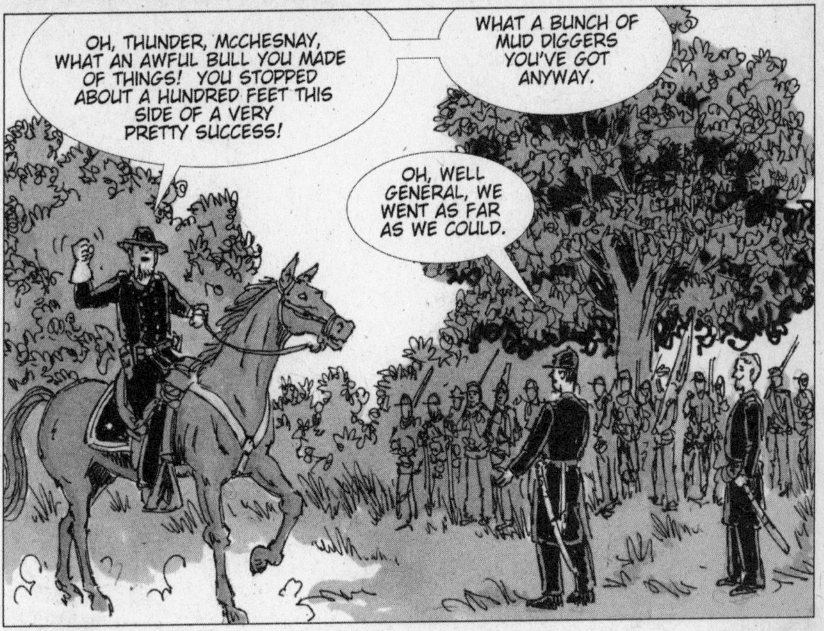
OH, THUNDER, MCCHESNAY, WHAT AN AWFUL BULL YOU MADE OF THINGS! YOU STOPPED ABOUT A HUNDRED FEET THIS SIDE OF A VERY PRETTY SUCCESS!
WHAT A BUNCH OF MUD DIGGERS YOU'VE GOT ANYWAY.
OH, WELL GENERAL, WE WENT AS FAR AS WE COULD.

HEARING THIS, THE YOUNG LIEUTENANT WAS IN AN IMPOTENT RAGE!

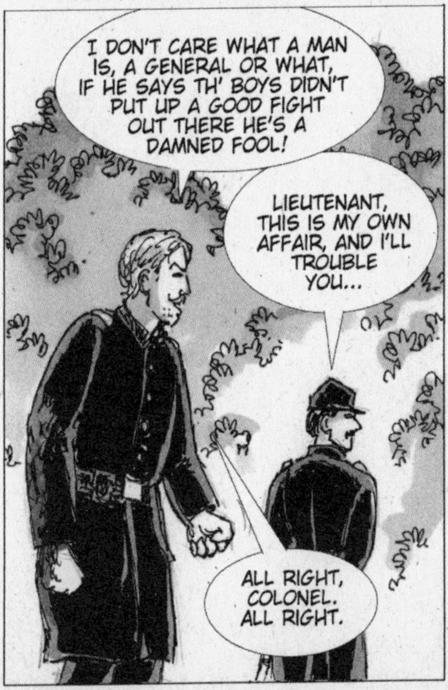
I DON'T CARE WHAT A MAN IS, A GENERAL OR WHAT, IF HE SAYS TH' BOYS DIDN'T PUT UP A GOOD FIGHT OUT THERE HE'S A DAMNED FOOL!
LIEUTENANT, THIS IS MY OWN AFFAIR, AND I'LL TROUBLE YOU...
ALL RIGHT, COLONEL. ALL RIGHT.

THE NEWS THAT THE REGIMENT HAD BEEN REPROACHED WENT ALONG THE LINE, AND THE MEN WERE BEWILDERED AND ANGRY.

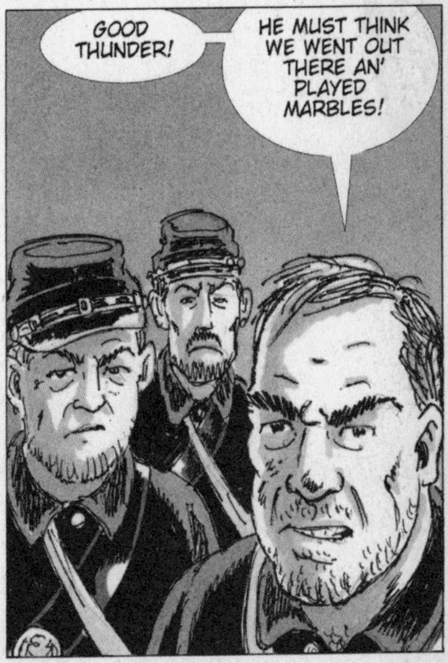
GOOD THUNDER!
HE MUST THINK WE WENT OUT THERE AN' PLAYED MARBLES!

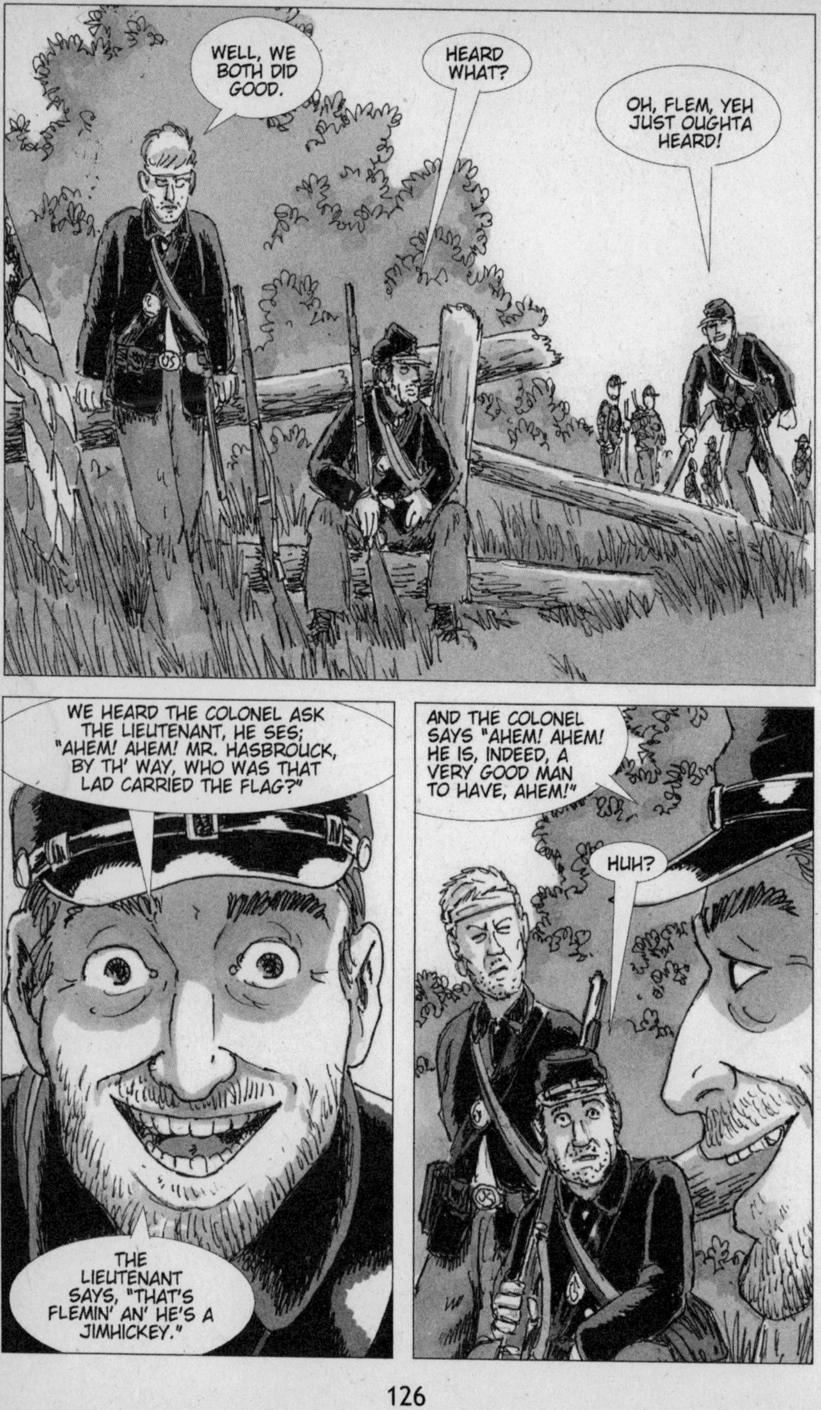
WELL, WE BOTH DID GOOD.
HEARD WHAT?
OH, FLEM, YEH JUST OUGHTA HEARD!
WE HEARD THE COLONEL ASK THE LIEUTENANT, HE SES; "AHEM! AHEM! MR. HASBROUCK, BY TH' WAY, WHO WAS THAT LAD CARRIED THE FLAG?"
THE LIEUTENANT SAYS, "THAT'S FLEMIN' AN' HE'S A JIMHICKEY."
AND THE COLONEL SAYS "AHEM! AHEM! HE IS, INDEED, A VERY GOOD MAN TO HAVE, AHEM!"
HUH?

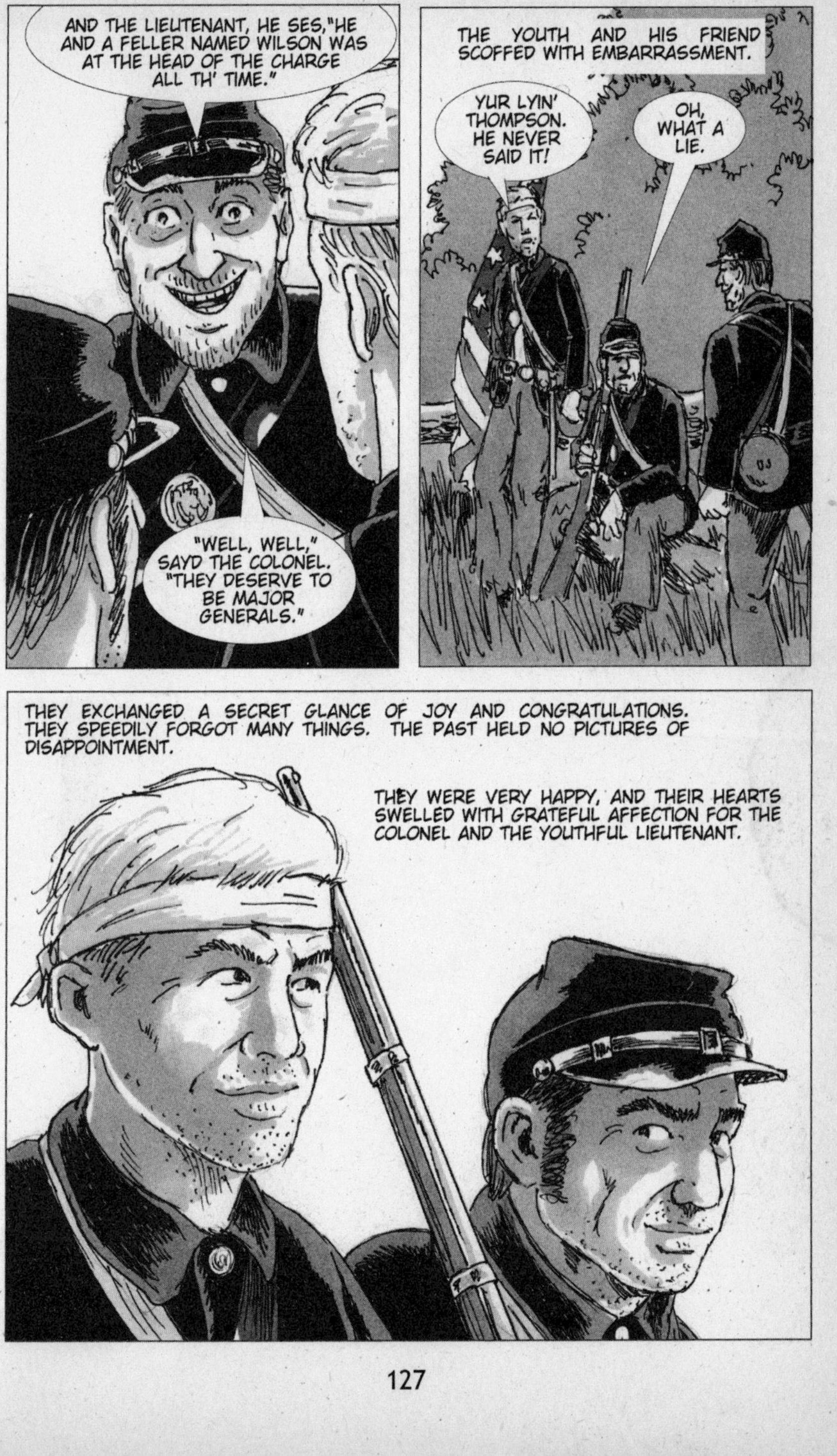
AND THE LIEUTENANT, HE SES, "HE AND A FELLER NAMED WILSON WAS AT THE HEAD OF THE CHARGE ALL TH' TIME."
"WELL, WELL," SAYD THE COLONEL. "THEY DESERVE TO BE MAJOR GENERALS."
THE YOUTH AND HIS FRIEND SCOFFED WITH EMBARRASSMENT.
YUR LYIN' THOMPSON. HE NEVER SAID IT!
OH, WHAT A LIE.
THEY EXCHANGED A SECRET GLANCE OF JOY AND CONGRATULATIONS. THEY SPEEDILY FORGOT MANY THINGS. THE PAST HELD NO PICTURES OF DISAPPOINTMENT.
THEY WERE VERY HAPPY, AND THEIR HEARTS SWELLED WITH GRATEFUL AFFECTION FOR THE COLONEL AND THE YOUTHFUL LIEUTENANT.

WHEN THE WOODS AGAIN BEGAN TO POUR FORTH THE DARK-HUED MASSES OF THE ENEMY THE YOUTH FELT SERENE SELF-CONFIDENCE. OFF A SHORT WAY HE SAW TWO REGIMENTS FIGHTING A LITTLE SEPARATE BATTLE WITH TWO OTHER REGIMENTS.

THE FOUR REGIMENTS WERE NOT INTERFERED WITH FROM ANY OUTSIDE DECISION OR INCLINATION: THEY SETTLED THEIR DISPUTE BY THEMSELVES. THEY STRUCK SAVAGELY AND POWERFULLY AT EACH OTHER FOR A PERIOD OF MINUTES, AND THEN THE LIGHTER-HUED REGIMENTS FALTERED AND DREW BACK, LEAVING THE DARK BLUE LINE SHOUTING.

THE YOUTH COULD SEE THE TWO FLAGS SHAKING WITH LAUGHTER AMID THE SMOKE REMNANTS.

SUDDENLY THE GUNS ON THE SLOPE ROARED OUT A MESSAGE OF WARNING. THE EMACIATED REGIMENT BUSTED FORTH WITH UNDIMINISHED FIERCENESS WHEN THE TIME CAME. WHEN ASSAULTED AGAIN BY BULLETS, THE MEN BURST OUT IN A BARBARIC CRY OF RAGE AND PAIN. THEY BENT THEIR HEADS IN AIMS OF INTENT HATRED BEHIND THE PROJECTED HAMMERS OF THEIR GUNS. THEIR RAMRODS CLANGED LOUD WITH FURY.

THE LIEUTENANT, AFTER HAVING HIS ARM BANDAGED, LET OUT STRINGS OF EXPLETIVES WHICH HE SWUNG LASHLIKE OVER THE BACKS OF HIS MEN.

THE YOUTH, STILL BEARER OF THE COLORS, DID NOT FEEL IDLENESS. HE WAS DEEPLY ABSORBED AS A SPECTATOR.

A FORMIDABLE LINE OF THE ENEMY CAME WITHIN DANGEROUS RANGE.

HE COULD BE SEEN PLAINLY — TALL, GAUNT MEN WITH EXCITED FACES RUNNING WITH LONG STRIDES TOWARD A WANDERING FENCE.

THE INSTANT THE MEN OF THE REGIMENT RECOGNIZED THE MENACE, THEY THREW UP THEIR RIFLES AND FIRED A PLUMPING VOLLEY AT THE FOE. THERE HAD BEEN NO ORDER GIVEN.

131

BUT THE ENEMY WAS QUICK TO GAIN THE PROTECTION OF THE LINE OF FENCE.
THEY SLID DOWN BEHIND IT WITH REMARKABLE CELERITY, AND FROM THIS
POSITION THEY BEGAN BRISKLY TO SLICE UP THE BLUE MEN.

THE BLUE REGIMENT BRACED THEIR ENERGIES FOR A GREAT STRUGGLE. THE
YOUTH RESOLVED NOT TO BUDGE WHATEVER HAPPENED. IT WAS CLEAR TO HIM
THAT HIS FINAL AND ABSOLUTE REVENGE WAS TO BE ACHIEVED BY HIS DEAD BODY
LYING, TORN AND GLITTERING, UPON THE FIELD.

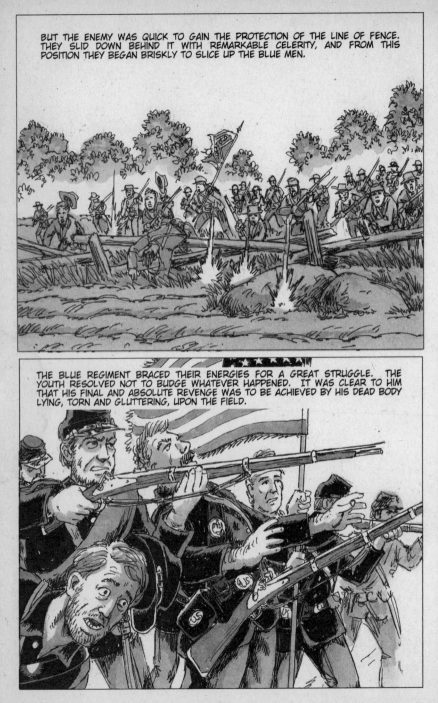

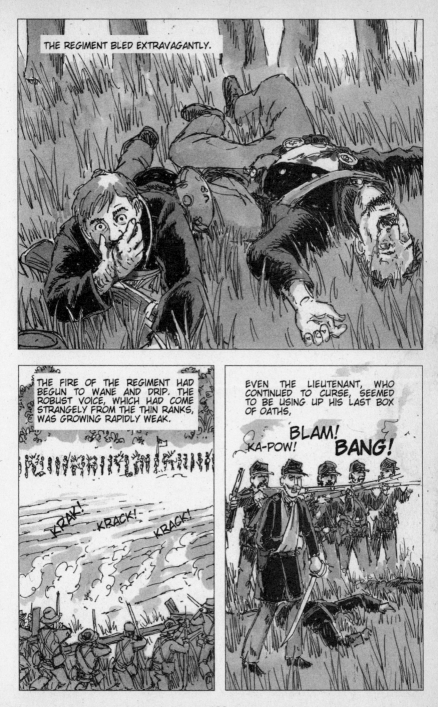

THE REGIMENT BLED EXTRAVAGANTLY.

THE FIRE OF THE REGIMENT HAD BEGUN TO WANE AND DRIP. THE ROBUST VOICE, WHICH HAD COME STRANGELY FROM THE THIN RANKS, WAS GROWING RAPIDLY WEAK.

KRAK!
KRACK!
KRACK!

EVEN THE LIEUTENANT, WHO CONTINUED TO CURSE, SEEMED TO BE USING UP HIS LAST BOX OF OATHS,

KA-POW!
BLAM!
BANG!

THE COLONEL CAME RUNNING ALONG THE BACK OF THE LINE:

WE MUST CHARGE'M!

WE MUST CHARGE'M!

IT WOULD BE DEATH TO STAY IN THE PRESENT PLACE, AND TO GO BACKWARDS WOULD EXALT TOO MANY OTHERS. HE EXPECTED THAT HIS COMPANIONS, WEARY AND STIFFENED, WOULD HAVE TO BE DRIVEN TO THE ASSAULT. BUT THERE WAS A NEW AND UNEXPECTED FORCE IN THE MOVEMENT OF THE REGIMENT. THEY WERE IN A STATE OF FRENZY.

IT APPEARED THAT THE SWIFT WINGS OF THEIR DESIRES WOULD HAVE SHATTERED THE IRON GATES OF THE IMPOSSIBLE.

THE YOUTH KEPT THE BRIGHT COLORS TO THE FRONT...

...AND CENTERED THE GAZE OF HIS SOUL UPON THE OTHER FLAG.

AS HE RAN A THOUGHT OF THE SHOCK OF CONTACT GLEAMED IN HIS MIND. HE EXPECTED A GREAT CONCUSSION WHEN THE TWO BODIES OF TROOPS CRASHED TOGETHER. IT SEEMED THAT IN TRUTH THERE WOULD BE A CLOSE AND FRIGHTFUL SCUFFLE.

THE MEN IN BLUE SHOWED THEIR TEETH.

BUT PRESENTLY HE COULD SEE THAT MANY OF THE MEN IN GRAY DID NOT INTEND TO ABIDE THE BLOW.

THE SWIRLING BODY OF BLUE MEN CAME TO A SUDDEN HALT AT CLOSE AND DISASTROUS RANGE AND ROARED A SWIFT VOLLEY.

KRAK!
KRACK!
KRACK!
KRACK!
KRACK!
KRAK!
KRACK!
KRACK!
KRACK!
KRAK!
KRAK!
KRAK!
KRAK!

THE GROUP IN GRAY WAS SPLIT AND BROKEN BY THIS FIRE, BUT ITS RIDDLED BODY STILL FOUGHT.

TOTTERING AMONG THEM WAS THE RIVAL COLOR BEARER WITH THE BLEACH OF DEATH OVERTAKING HIS FACE.

THE MEN IN BLUE YELLED AGAIN AND RUSHED IN UPON THEM. THE YOUTH'S FRIEND WENT OVER THE OBSTRUCTION IN A TUMBLING HEAP.

HE SPRANG AT THE FLAG AS A PANTHER AT PREY. HE PULLED AT IT AND, WRENCHING IT FREE, SWUNG UP ITS RED BRILLIANCY WITH A MAD CRY OF EXULTATION.

THE COLOR BEARER, GASPING, LURCHED OVER IN A FINAL THROE AND, STIFFENING CONVULSIVELY, TURNED HIS HEAD FACE TO THE GROUND.

THERE WAS MUCH BLOOD UPON THE GRASS.

AT ONE PART OF THE LINE FOUR MEN HAD BEEN SWOOPED UPON, AND THEY NOW SAT AS PRISONERS. ONE WAS NURSING A WOUND IN THE FOOT. HE CUDDLED IT, BABY-WISE, BUT HE LOOKED UP FROM IT OFTEN TO CURSE WITH AN ASTONISHING UTTER ABANDON AT THE NOSES OF HIS CAPTORS.

ANOTHER, WHO WAS A BOY IN YEARS, TOOK HIS PLIGHT WITH GREAT CALMNESS AND APPARENT GOOD NATURE. HE CONVERSED WITH THE MEN IN BLUE, STUDYING THEIR FACES WITH BRIGHT AND KEEN EYES.

THE THIRD CAPTIVE PRESERVED A STOICAL AND COLD ATTITUDE. TO ALL ADVANCES HE MADE ONE REPLY WITHOUT VARIATION, "AH, GO T' HELL!"

THE LAST OF THE FOUR WAS ALWAYS SILENT AND, FOR THE MOST PART, KEPT HIS FACE TURNED IN UNMOLESTED DIRECTIONS. IT LOOKED LIKE SHAME WAS UPON HIM, AND WITH IT PROFOUND REGRET THAT HE WAS, PERHAPS, NO MORE TO BE COUNTED IN THE RANKS OF HIS FELLOWS.

THERE WAS SOME LONG GRASS. THE YOUTH NESTLED IN IT AND RESTED, MAKING A CONVENIENT RAIL TO SUPPORT THE FLAG.

HE BEGAN TO STUDY HIS DEEDS, HIS FAILURES AND ACHIEVEMENTS.

THE GHOST OF HIS FLIGHT FROM THE FIRST ENGAGEMENT APPEARED TO HIM AND DANCED.

THERE WERE SMALL SHOUTINGS IN HIS BRAIN ABOUT THESE MATTERS. FOR A MOMENT HE BLUSHED, AND THE LIGHT OF HIS SOUL FLICKERED WITH SHAME.

YET GRADUALLY HE MUSTERED FORCE TO PUT THE SIN AT A DISTANCE,

HIS FRIEND, JUBILANT AND GLORIFIED, HOLDING HIS TREASURE WITH VANITY, CAME TO HIM THERE.

WELL, WHAT NOW I WONDER?

I BET WE'RE GOIN' T' GIT ALONG OUT OF THIS AN' BACK OVER TH' RIVER.

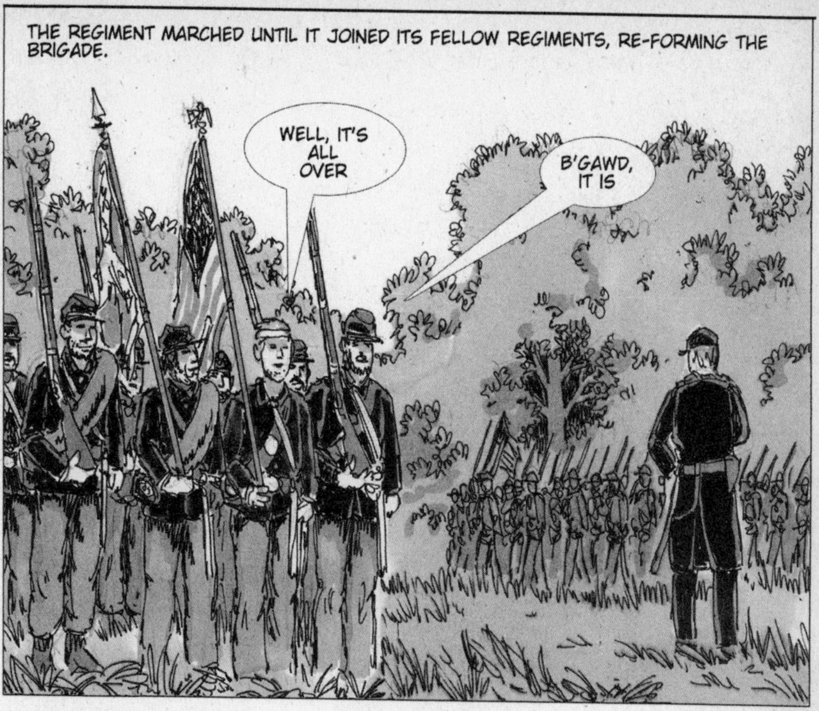
THE REGIMENT MARCHED UNTIL IT JOINED ITS FELLOW REGIMENTS, RE-FORMING THE BRIGADE.
WELL, IT'S ALL OVER
B'GAWD, IT IS

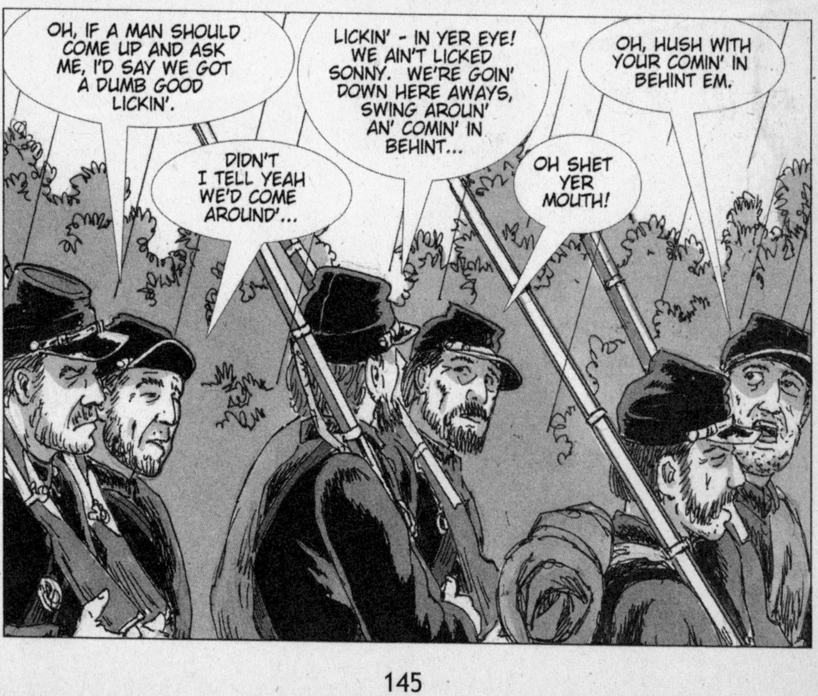
OH, IF A MAN SHOULD COME UP AND ASK ME, I'D SAY WE GOT A DUMB GOOD LICKIN'.
DIDN'T I TELL YEAH WE'D COME AROUND'...
LICKIN' - IN YER EYE! WE AIN'T LICKED SONNY. WE'RE GOIN' DOWN HERE AWAYS, SWING AROUN' AN' COMIN' IN BEHINT...
OH SHET YER MOUTH!
OH, HUSH WITH YOUR COMIN' IN BEHINT EM.

IT RAINED. THE PROCESSION OF WEARY SOLDIERS BECAME A BEDRAGGLED TRAIN, DESPONDENT AND MUTTERING, MARCHING WITH CHURNING EFFORT IN A TROUGH OF LIQUID BROWN.

SO IT CAME TO PASS THAT AS HE TRUDGED FROM THE PLACE OF BLOOD AND WRATH HIS SOUL CHANGED. SCARS FADED AS FLOWERS. HE HAD BEEN TO SEE THE GREAT DEATH, AND FOUND THAT, AFTER ALL IT WAS BUT THE GREAT DEATH.

HE WAS A MAN.

146

THE YOUTH SMILED, FOR HE SAW THAT THE WORLD WAS A WORLD FOR HIM...

...THOUGH MANY DISCOVERED IT TO BE MADE OF OATHS AND WALKING STICKS.

HE HAD RID HIMSELF OF THE RED SICKNESS OF BATTLE. THE SULTRY NIGHTMARE WAS IN THE PAST.

HE HAD BEEN AN ANIMAL BLISTERING AND SWEATING IN THE HEAT AND PAIN OF WAR.

HE TURNED NOW WITH A LOVER'S THIRST TO IMAGES OF TRANQUIL SKIES, FRESH MEADOWS, COOL BROOKS...AN EXISTENCE OF SOFT AND ETERNAL PEACE.

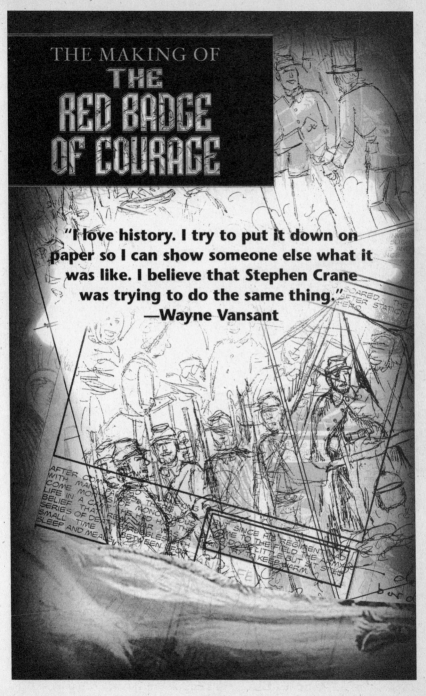

THE MAKING OF
THE RED BADGE OF COURAGE

"I love history. I try to put it down on paper so I can show someone else what it was like. I believe that Stephen Crane was trying to do the same thing."
—Wayne Vansant

Wayne Vansant talks about his adaptation of

STEPHEN CRANE'S
THE
RED BADGE
OF COURAGE

Stories of the American Civil War have their own rules of comics layout and design. If you've ever been to a big Civil War re-enactment (where there are as many as 10,000 men in uniform) you can imagine how majestic, awe-inspiring and *terrible* these occasions were. Hundreds, even thousands of men fought together in close proximity.

Although there was much smoke from the weapons of the time, you cannot cheat and show a few obscure figures in a panel.You must draw many dissimilar men, in ragged, fearful rows. Sometimes, there uniforms will be "uniform" as with the Federals, and not as often with the Confederates.

Each battle was different. In the case of *The Red Badge of Courage*, the young Henry Fleming and his comrades are in a untried regiment of the Army of the Potomac. Their uniforms would be new and they would all be wearing the little blue kepis so prevalent in that army. If the story had the Union Army of the Tennessee attacking Atlanta in 1864, the men in blue would all be bearded and wearing slouch hats, carring very little personal gear—a few might even be barefoot! Depending on the battle, the Confederates could be in a wide variety of uniforms, from frock coats to shell jackets, and in colors from dark, blue-gray to light yellowish butternut.

The Puffin Classics edition of *The Red Badge of Courage*
that was the source for Wayne's adaptation.

The best way to present a plot summary is by doing an outline of "scenes" or "acts."

A. In the Union camp by the river.
  1. The Tall Soldier runs back from washing his shirt with the news that the Army is to "Move."
  2. Argument of the soldiers: "It's a lie. That's all it is..."
  3. Introduction of the "Youth", Henry Fleming, who is not taking part in the discussion.
  4. Henry walks back to his hut.
  5. Henry flashbacks to home.
    a. Dreams of glorious warfare (wearing shining armor)
    b. Tells his mother he wants to enlist. Her reply: "Don't be a fool, Henry."
    c. Henry enlist anyway.
    d. He tells his mother what he did. "The Lord's will be done, Henry."
    e. His mother's advice to him as he prepares to leave.
    f. His visit to the seminary (school): His friends and the light-haired and dark-haired girls.
    g. The road to Washington and how exciting it was.
    h. On sentry duty, talking to the rebel pickett across the river.
  6. Back at the hut, the Tall Soldier and the Loud Soldier enter:
    a. They discuss, "How the regiment will do."
    b. And, "Think any of the boys'll run?"

A copy of a page of Wayne's plot breakdown of the story.

HOW WAYNE WORKS:
Pencil Art

For penciling, I use a 0.5mm HB lead. The paper I like is bristol board with a smooth finish. But if I'm adding color or gray tones on the art, I prefer to use paper that allows a little more bleed so the colors or gray tones will smooth out a little.

When I work in black and white, I like to use a wash gray tone. Years ago, I used a lot of craft-tint duo-shade paper. This is a bristol board with two invisible line patterns printed on the paper that become visible with the application of a clear solution. I've always liked the look of duo-shade, but the paper is very expensive and the tone range is limited.

A rough pencil sketch, the first step in the creation of Wayne's art.

The next step: the pencil art is more tightly drawn and
has more detail.

HOW WAYNE WORKS:
Inking

I ink primarily with a Sanford Uni-ball micro pen. I've experimented over the years with quill pens, Rapdiographs, and brushes. For me the Uni-ball is just fine. It's smooth and fast. It sometimes gives a line that is rough and scratchy looking, but that fits if my story is historical or about combat. I fill in the larger areas with Alvin Penstix 0.7mm and different sizes of Sanford Sharpies.

The first step in the inking and toning process. An inked illustration of the soldier.

HOW WAYNE WORKS:
Toning

For gray tones, like what I'm doing on *The Red Badge of Courage,* I use Tria cool gray markers #1 through #10. I apply the grays right onto the inked pages. Right now, I am experimenting with a new process where I apply the gray markers right onto tight pencil drawing. To me this conveys an almost photographic reality. I'm always trying something new; you can never stop learning.

The first step in the toning. Note how flat the gray areas appear.

The finished drawing of the soldier. Note that the gray
areas have different levels of intensity, and there is some
shading on the hat and the shirt.

THE LOST SEQUENCE

One of the advantages of seeing a story breakdown in the pencil sketch stage is that revisions are easy to do. Here is a rare opportunity to see the first version of one of the battle sequences, beginning on page thirty-one. What follows is a reproduction of Wayne's pencils and script along with the editorial notes. Compare this sequence to the revised version printed in the story. Note, the term "float caption" means that the caption text should not have a border.

The original sketch for page 31. Handwritten editorial comments are on the right.

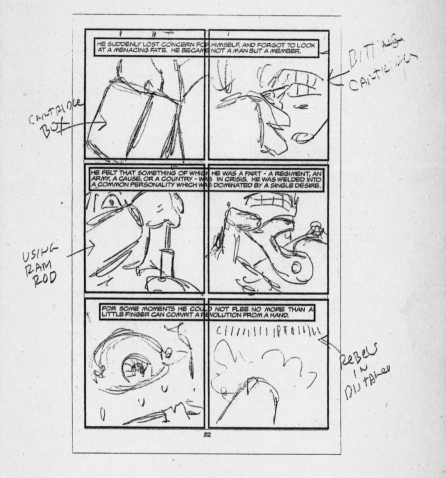

The handwritten notes identify the illustration and action in the panel. Other notes on the following pages also deal with text changes.

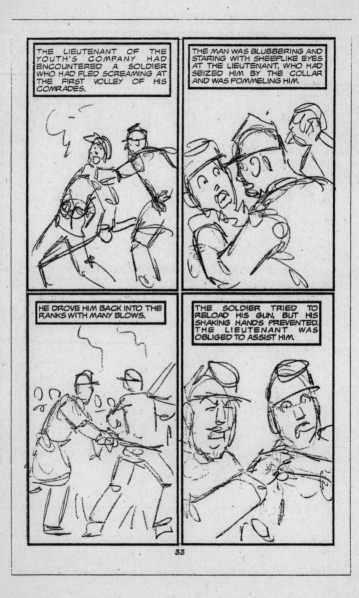

THE LIEUTENANT OF THE YOUTH'S COMPANY HAD ENCOUNTERED A SOLDIER WHO HAD FLED SCREAMING AT THE FIRST VOLLEY OF HIS COMRADES.

THE MAN WAS BLUBBERING AND STARING WITH SHEEPLIKE EYES AT THE LIEUTENANT, WHO HAD SEIZED HIM BY THE COLLAR AND WAS POMMELING HIM.

HE DROVE HIM BACK INTO THE RANKS WITH MANY BLOWS.

THE SOLDIER TRIED TO RELOAD HIS GUN, BUT HIS SHAKING HANDS PREVENTED. THE LIEUTENANT WAS OBLIGED TO ASSIST HIM.

33

164

Make this
a full-page
illustration

AT LAST AN EXULTANT YELL WENT ALONG THE QUIVERING LINE. THE FIRING DWINDLED FROM AN UPROAR TO A LAST VINDICTIVE POPPING.

AS THE SMOKE SLOWLY EDDIED AWAY, THE YOUTH SAW THAT THE CHARGE HAD BEEN REPULSED. THE ENEMY WERE SCATTERED INTO RELUCTANT GROUPS.

SOME OF THE REGIMENT BEGAN TO WHOOP FRENZIEDLY. MANY WERE SILENT. APPARENTLY THEY WERE TRYING TO CONTEMPLATE THEMSELVES.

35

MAKE EACH PANEL A FULL-PAGE ILLUSTRATION

FLOAT THE CAPTIONS

UNION LINE

CONFEDERATES FALLING BACK

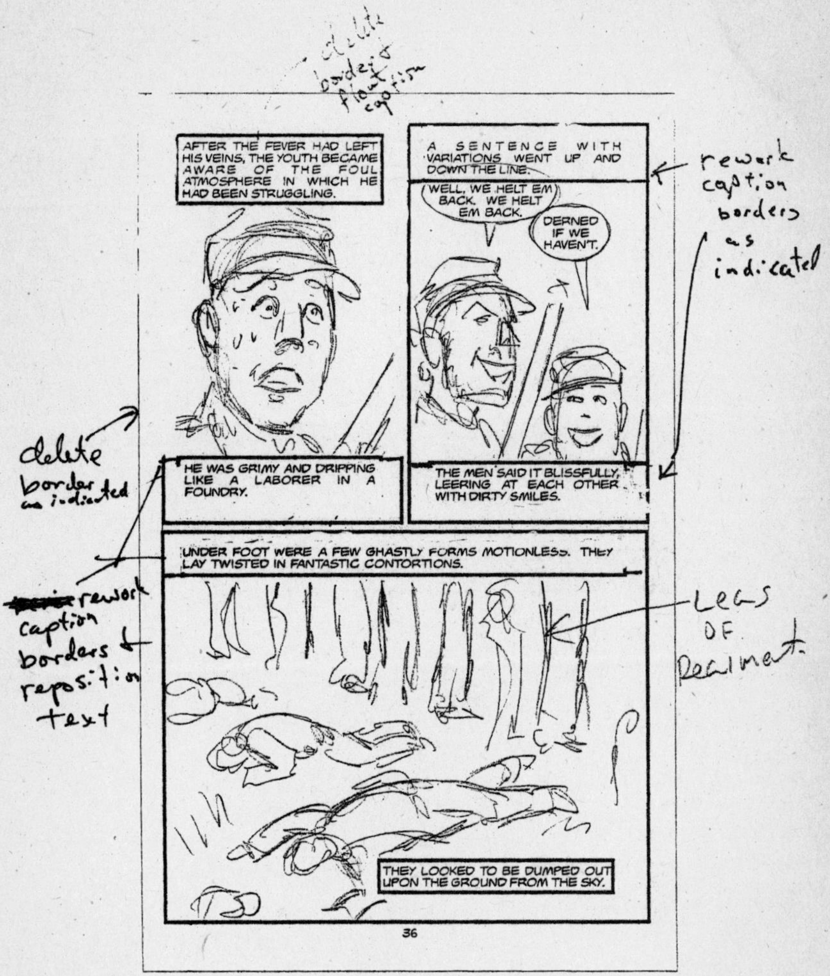
delete border & float caption
AFTER THE FEVER HAD LEFT HIS VEINS, THE YOUTH BECAME AWARE OF THE FOUL ATMOSPHERE IN WHICH HE HAD BEEN STRUGGLING.
A SENTENCE WITH VARIATIONS WENT UP AND DOWN THE LINE.
WELL, WE HELT EM BACK. WE HELT EM BACK.
DERNED IF WE HAVEN'T.
rework caption borders as indicated
delete border as indicated
HE WAS GRIMY AND DRIPPING LIKE A LABORER IN A FOUNDRY.
THE MEN SAID IT BLISSFULLY, LEERING AT EACH OTHER WITH DIRTY SMILES.
UNDER FOOT WERE A FEW GHASTLY FORMS MOTIONLESS. THEY LAY TWISTED IN FANTASTIC CONTORTIONS.
rework caption borders & reposition text
LEGS OF Regiment.
THEY LOOKED TO BE DUMPED OUT UPON THE GROUND FROM THE SKY.
36

THE YOUTH AWAKENED SLOWLY.

SO IT WAS ALL OVER AT LAST! THE SUPREME TRIAL HAD BEEN PASSED. THE RED, FORMIDABLE DIFFICULTIES OF WAR HAD BEEN VANQUISHED.

reposition & float caption

HE HAD THE MOST DELIGHTFUL SENSATIONS OF HIS LIFE. STANDING AS IF APART FROM HIMSELF, HE VIEWED THAT LAST SCENE. HE PERCEIVED THAT THE MAN WHO HAD FOUGHT THUS WAS MAGNIFICENT.

reposition caption

HE FELT LIKE HE WAS A FINE FELLOW. HE SAW HIMSELF EVEN WITH THOSE IDEALS WHICH HE HAD CONSIDERED BEYOND HIM. HE SMILED IN DEEP GRATIFICATION.

reposition caption

37

168

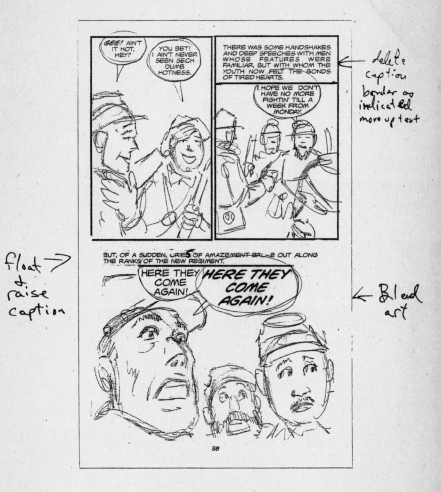

delete
caption
border as
indicated
move up text

float →
&
raise
caption

← Bleed
art

THE YOUTH TURNED QUICK EYES UPON THE FIELD. HE DISCERNED FORMS BEGIN TO SWELL IN MASSES OUT OF A DISTANT WOOD. HE AGAIN SAW THE TILTED FLAG SPEEDING FORWARD.

Bleed
art

39

THE MEN GROANED. THE LUSTER FADED FROM THEIR EYES. THEIR SMUDGED COUNTENANCES NOW EXPRESSED A PROFOUND DEJECTION.

OH, SAY, THIS IS TOO MUCH OF A GOOD THING...

...WHY CAN'T SOMEBODY SEND US SUPPORTERS?

THE YOUTH STARED. SURELY, HE THOUGHT, THIS IMPOSSIBLE THING WAS NOT ABOUT TO HAPPEN. HE WAITED AS IF HE EXPECTED THE ENEMY TO SUDDENLY STOP, APOLOGIZE, AND RETIRE BOWING. IT WAS ALL A *MISTAKE*.

TO THE YOUTH IT WAS AN ONSLAUGHT OF REDOUBTABLE DRAGONS. HE BECAME LIKE THE MAN WHO LOST HIS LEGS AT THE APPROACH OF THE RED AND GREEN MONSTER.

A MAN NEAR HIM WHO UP TO THIS TIME HAD BEEN WORKING FEVERISHLY A HIS RIFLE SUDDENLY STOPPED AND RAN WITH HOWLS.

40

171

Panel 1: A LAD WHOSE FACE HAD BORNE AN EXPRESSION OF EXALTED COURAGE, THREW DOWN HIS GUN AND FLED. THERE WAS A REVELATION. THERE WAS NO SHAME ON HIS FACE.

...HE RAN LIKE A RABBIT..

Panel 2: OTHERS BEGAN TO SCAMPER AWAY THROUGH THE SMOKE. HE SAW THE FEW FLEETING FORMS.

Panel 3: HE YELLED THEN WITH FRIGHT AND SWUNG ABOUT.

Panel 4: FOR A MOMENT, HE LOST THE DIRECTION OF SAFETY. DESTRUCTION THREATENED HIM FROM ALL POINTS.

reposition caption

float caption

reposition caption

41

DIRECTLY HE BEGAN TO SPEED TOWARD THE REAR IN GREAT LEAPS. HIS RIFLE AND CAP WERE GONE. HIS UNBUTTONED COAT BULGED IN THE WIND. THE FLAP OF HIS CARTRIDGE BOX BOBBED WILDLY, AND HIS CANTEEN, BY ITS SLENDER CORD, SWUNG OUT BEHIND.

DESTRUCTION THREATENEN HIM FROM ALL POINTS.

HE RAN LIKE A BLIND MAN. TWO OR THREE TIMES HE FELL DOWN. ONCE HE KNOCKED HIS SHOULDER SO HEAVILY AGAINST A TREE THAT HE WENT HEADLONG.

42

float captions

Float caption & more text down

STEPHEN CRANE (1871-1900) wrote only a few books, not all of which were successful; yet he is universally acknowledged as one of the giants of American literature.

When *The Red Badge of Courage* was published in 1895, no one had heard of Crane, yet here was a work of mature genius. Though Crane had no experience on the battlefield, his daily hardships as an impoverished writer living in New York, as well as his numerous interviews with Civil War veterans, enabled him to write *The Red Badge of Courage*, considered one of the most brilliant and profound war books ever written. The book's chief merits are the intensity of its writing, the sensitivity of its insights into human emotion, and the brilliance of its descriptions. Crane's vivid and astonishingly realistic portrayal of the horrors of war, won him notoriety as an exceptional writer, particularly on the topic of war. Several newspapers became interested in Crane's talents and hired him as a war correspondent.

In 1897, Crane made a fateful journey aboard an American expedition to Cuba. On the way there, his ship was wrecked and Crane spent four days in a lifeboat, drifting in the Atlantic Ocean. The event inspired him to write "The Open Boat," which has been called the finest short story written in English. The experience also resulted in the permanent impairment of Crane's health.

Crane moved to England in late 1897, where he befriended the writers Joseph Conrad and fellow American expatriate, Henry James. Before his death at age twenty-nine of tuberculosis, Crane published *Whilomville Stories*, the last and at the time, most successful book of his writing career.

DON TROIANI (cover) has been universally acclaimed for the accuracy, drama, and sensitivity of his paintings of America's past, particularly the Civil War. Troiani attended the Pennsylvania Academy of Fine Arts and New York City's Art Students League. His artwork is in numerous collections, including those of *American Heritage* magazine, the National Park Service, West Point Military Academy, The National Civil War Museum, Parks of Canada, the Pentagon, and museums such as the Smithsonian Institute. His illustrations have appeared on the cover of *Gettysburg Magazine* and inside both *American Heritage* and *Smithsonian* magazines, in television productions by NBC, CNN, and the Arts & Entertainment Network, and on books published by Time-Life and Stackpole Books. Troiani was the advisor on History Channel's *Civil War Journal* and the miniseries *The American Revolution.* He was the consultant on the feature film *Cold Mountain* starring Nicole Kidman, Renée Zellweger, and Jude Law.

WAYNE VANSANT was born in Atlanta, Georgia in 1949. He served in the US Navy during the Vietnam War and graduated from the Atlanta College of Art in 1975. His first war comic works appeared in Marvel's *Savage Tales* followed by *The 'Nam*, for which he wrote more than fifty stories.He also contributed to *Two Fisted Tales* Since then he has written and illustrated many comics and books on military subjects. He lives in Powder Springs, Georgia.

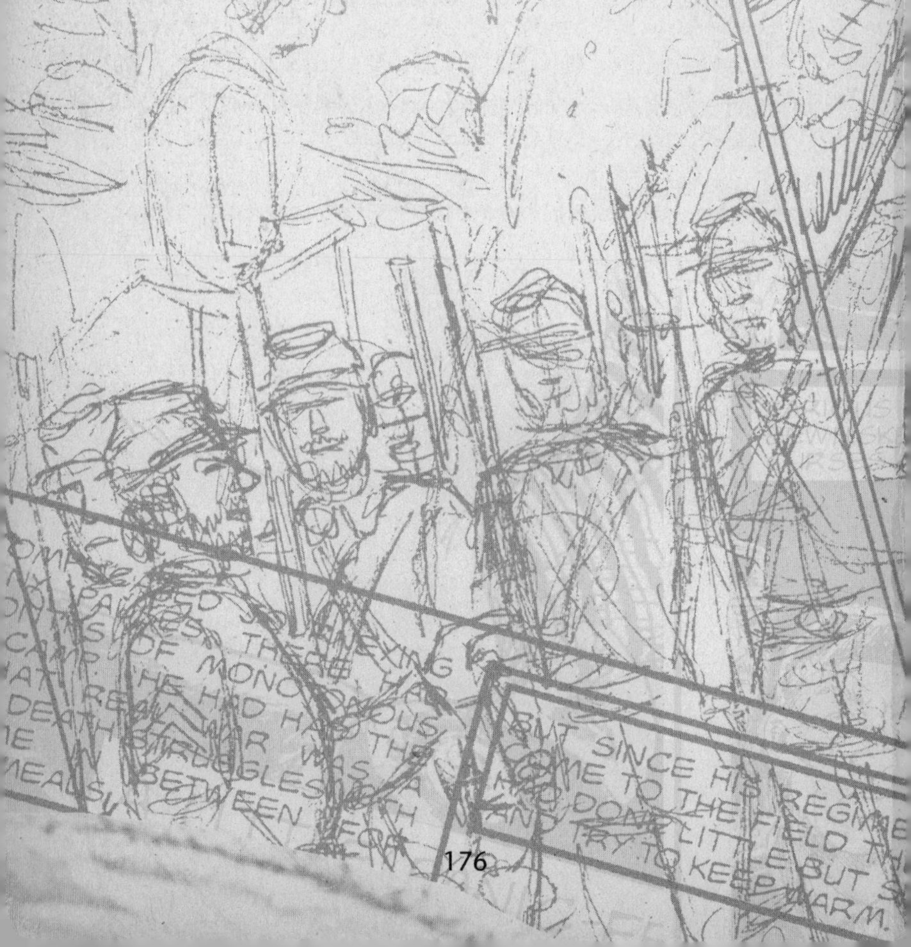